THE HOLY TERRORS

KU-244-155

By the same author

The Dadhunters

THE HOLY TERRORS

JOSEPHINE FEENEY

((Collins

An imprint of HarperCollinsPublishers

First published in hardback in Great Britain by Collins 2000
First published in paperback by Collins 2001
Collins is an imprint of HarperCollins*Publishers* Ltd
77-85 Fulham Palace Road, Hammersmith,
London, W6 8JB

The HarperCollins website address is:
www.**fireandwater**.com

1 3 5 7 9 8 6 4 2

Text copyright © Josephine Feeney 2000

ISBN 0 00 675533 X

The author asserts the moral right to be
Identified as the author of the work.

Printed and bound in Great Britain by
Omnia Books Limited, Glasgow

Conditions of Sale
This book is sold subject to the condition that it shall not, by way of trade or
otherwise, be lent, re-sold, hired out or otherwise circulated without
the publisher's prior written consent in any form of binding or cover other
than that in which it is published and without a similar condition including
this condition being imposed on the subsequent purchaser.

For Ruairi McKay,
my own Holy Terror

ONE

This is a story with a happy beginning. For Gary McNab, the conqueror of the Brecon Beacons, and Robert, (his friend), a dream had come true. Their scheming had worked. Happiness all around.

"That's it then," Robert said. "The Dadhunters found a dad!"

"Yes, that's it," Gary said. The best friends were sitting together on Robert's bedroom floor. "We found a dad."

"What does the letter actually say?" Robert asked.

Gary read the card out slowly and quietly.

7

Bernadette and Eugene
would like all their friends to know
that they were remarried today,
Friday 7th September,
in the beautiful city of Rome.

"That's all it says," Gary added.

"So – it's a happy ending, Gary. We planned and schemed for this and it's happened!" Robert said.

"Yes, I know," Gary mumbled.

"Why aren't you happy?" Robert probed.

"I'm happy," Gary said. But he wasn't.

"You're not. I can tell you're not. What's up?"

"I am happy."

"You're not," Robert said again.

"I am," Gary said but his face refused to be moved into a smile.

Gary and Robert were Dadhunters. They had tried to find a husband for Gary's mum. It was a long story.

This is Gary's explanation list:

1 Gary's mum and dad got divorced

2 Gary's dad was going to marry Karen

3 *Gary hated Karen*

4 *Gary was so worried that his mum might marry someone else he hated that Robert and Gary came up with a scheme*

5 *The boys would find a husband for her*

6 *Robert's Gran gave them advice about match-making – finding a husband for Gary's mum*

7 *First, they tried Mr Doyle, their teacher. He wasn't married and he was mad on football – an ideal candidate – and he seemed to like Bernadette, Gary's mum*

8 *This didn't work so the boys tried two other men*

9 *One they found through a dating agency*

10 *The other was a famous footballer. It was disastrous. Gary doesn't talk about it much, even though Robert finds it funny*

11 *In the end, Gary's dad, Eugene, broke up with*

*Karen and moved back home. He didn't choose
to move back in with Gary and Bernadette, he
just had nowhere else to go*

12 *Gary found it difficult at first but then they were
like a family once more. Now this, the happy
beginning – Gary's mum and dad had got
married again. In Rome!*

(Gary liked compiling lists especially when they
ended in round numbers like twelve.)

He should have been happy. Gary didn't know
how to start saying this to Robert because he was
big and strong but ... he missed his mum and dad.
He wanted to be with them. They were a family.
Families do important things together. Like getting
married. Why didn't they take him to Rome with
them? It wasn't a happy beginning for Gary. He felt
left out, excluded.

"Cheer up," Robert said, sensing Gary's gloom.
"They'll probably bring you a brilliant pressie back
from Italy."

"What, like a bag of pasta?" Gary said.

"No, don't be daft! Like the latest Italian football
strip," Robert suggested.

That wasn't the point. Gary wanted to be there, with them.

Gary stayed with Robert for ten days while his mum and dad got married again, in Italy. He didn't know they'd gone to Italy to get married. They said they were going on holiday. It was supposed to have been a break from everyone, and everything. He didn't understand why they didn't get married in Pocklington's Walk, like most people, or even at church. He could have *been* there. He was very upset about that.

When Robert was busy on the computer, Gary read the separate letter his mum and dad had written especially for him.

Rome,
Italy

Dear Gary,

We know you'll be thrilled when you get this news. You might have lots of questions, too, but we'll answer those when we arrive back home next week.

The main thing is, this is a new beginning for us, a happy beginning. We're a family again. After all we've been through, this is a fresh start.

What the future holds, we don't know, we can only guess. Maybe there will be brothers and sisters for you and lots of other wonderful things for us all to enjoy. City might even win the league!

Be happy with us, Gary. We love you. We miss you.

Mum and Dad

"Brothers and *sisters*?" Gary said, in amazement, his face was curled up in disgust.

"What?" Robert asked, turning from his computer game.

"You won't believe this, Robert..."

TWO

Friends and neighbours had two days to arrange a little surprise for Gary's mum and dad on their return from Italy. "A little impromptu wedding reception," Robert's gran suggested.

Gran had the keys to the house so she was able to let the 'decorators' in. When Bernadette and Eugene finally arrived home, the house was full of balloons and congratulations banners.

Gary watched from his bedroom window as Mum climbed out of the taxi and covered her smile with her hands as she shrieked, "I don't believe it!" Dad was busy paying the driver and unloading their luggage.

They weren't expecting such a welcome home.

Gary and Robert dropped home-made confetti from the bedroom window as the newlyweds walked into the house. The hall was lined with well-wishers; neighbours who'd been delighted to hear of the wedding. "It's what was meant to be," they agreed.

"What do you think, Dad?" Gary asked as he ran down the stairs to hug his parents.

"Whose idea was this?" Mum asked, still smiling broadly from the happy surprise.

"Robert's gran. She said you did us out of a wedding reception..." Gary began.

"Give us a big hug, Gary. We've missed you," Mum said, slightly tearful. The 'new' family stood, at the bottom of the stairs, with their arms wrapped around one another. The rest of the house clapped and clapped.

It was the best moment of Gary's life, well ... the best for a long time. Mum and Dad were crying, tears of happiness which Gary tried to wipe away for them.

"This is absolutely perfect," Mum said, through the tears. "Us three, back together again. A family once more."

Then the handshakes, the embraces and the

congratulations continued. It was a great, great party, a wonderful day. Eugene was smiling and carefree. The music bounced against the walls and up the stairs as Bernadette and Eugene moved from the front room to the back room, retelling their story several times.

As the neighbours began to drift away, back to their normal Saturday evening activities, Mum proclaimed, "Presents!"

"Oh yes, wait 'til you see what we've brought you, Gary."

"You shouldn't have, Dad," Gary said, mocking his parents who had said it several times that evening each time they'd been presented with a wedding gift.

"Here you are," Dad said, as he produced a package from his hand luggage.

Gary unwrapped it quickly. "Wow! A Lazio top!"

"Glad you like it, son. We went to the Lazio stadium, incredible isn't it, love?" Eugene said.

"Yes," Mum replied, rolling her eyes. "Though it wasn't quite as good as the Colosseum or the Forum."

"And here's a present for Robert," Mum said,

flourishing another small package.

"And here's one for you, Mrs Keane," Dad said to Robert's gran.

"You shouldn't have," Robert's gran protested.

"Thanks for looking after our little treasure," Mum said, ruffling Gary's hair.

"You're more than welcome," Gran replied. "He's a great boy. You'll never get another one like Gary, you know," Gran said.

"We know. We're very lucky," Gary's mum agreed.

"What is it? What have you got, Gran?" Robert asked.

"Oh lovely," Gran said. "It's some pasta. Thanks."

Robert and Gary giggled loudly. "A bag of pasta!" they chorused.

"It isn't just a bag of pasta, it's rainbow pasta and we had it in a restaurant one night and it was absolutely delicious. You can do it with a basil sauce or something like that," Mum suggested.

"Shall we try it tonight, Robert?" Gran asked. Robert was still giggling. "OK Robert. I think party time's over now. We ought to be making our way home."

"There's a recipe suggestion on the back of the packet," Mum said. "Oh ... and we've brought some wine for you, too."

"And a signed picture of the Pope and some smelly Italian cheese," Dad said. "Gary is always talking about your brilliant cooking."

"I'm more of a cake woman, myself," Gran said. "But thanks for these goodies, all the same. Now, come on, Robert," Gran insisted.

Robert reluctantly left with his Gran. Eugene and Bernadette sat amidst their unpacked bags for ages, talking about all that they had seen and done in Rome.

"What did you think when you got the letter, Gary?" Mum asked suddenly.

"I dunno," Gary said, shrugging his shoulders.

"You didn't ... mind, did you?" Eugene probed.

"No," Gary said, uncertainly.

"Are you sure?" Dad asked again.

"Go on, Gary. Tell us the truth," Mum said.

"I did a bit. I did mind," Gary replied.

"I thought you would," Mum said, a little deflated. "I told you, Eugene. I said Gary might be upset."

"But you're not now, are you son? Everything's

fine now, isn't it?" Dad asked.

"No, yes, I'm fine," Gary said.

"What's the matter?" Mum questioned. "There's something the matter, isn't there?"

"What did you mean about brothers and sisters?" Gary asked.

"What did we ... ummm, what did we write?" Dad replied.

"That there might be some. That's what you said."

"Did we?" Mum asked. "Well, you never know."

"But it's perfect with just us three," Gary said.

"I know Gary but it could be even better."

"How?" Gary said. He wanted to say that it was impossible to improve on perfect.

"I'll tell you how," suggested Dad. "After a wonderful holiday in Italy, a brilliant welcome home, a fantastic son and – Match of the Day is on in ten minutes!"

"Yess!" Gary shouted. "I'll just change into my Lazio shirt."

And so, any mention of babies was banished from the McNab household. For the moment.

THREE

Gary just couldn't stop thinking about the prospect of babies – or rather, *any* baby, in his house. When things were almost back to normal, he confided in Robert again.

"Don't worry about that," Robert said. "Leave it to me. I'll sort something out." Gary had every confidence in his best friend. He was so good at sorting things out.

"How do you stop people having babies, Gran?" Robert asked her the next day. She looked blankly round the table where Gary and Robert sat, in their new Lazio tops, eating the most delicious lemon cake ever made. The kitchen fell totally silent.

"Ask your mum," Robert's gran suggested.

"Why? Why can't you tell us? You told us about the matchmaking, why can't you tell us about this? That's what everyone says, 'Why can't you ask your mum?'" Robert said indignantly.

"That's the sort of thing your mum tells you," Gran said. "Now eat up, boys. I want to get this place cleaned up early today. Anyways, who else have you asked?"

"Oh ... just Mr Doyle and Ronan," Gary replied. Ronan was Robert's stepfather.

Gran's eyebrows rose at the thought of Ronan getting this question. "And what, exactly, did Ronan say?" she asked.

"He told us not to be so cheeky. He swore," Gary responded in between huge mouthfuls of cake.

"Now tell me, why would you want to know something like that, boys?"

"Because, because..." Robert began.

"That's what they said, Mum and Dad. In the letter – they said about brothers and sisters..." Gary stammered. "They even talked about it that day when they got home." Robert's gran looked confused. "And then I heard them talking about it. They didn't know I was there in the kitchen, making hot chocolate and listening."

"So ... what exactly did they say?" Robert's gran inquired, getting drawn into Gary's problem.

"I heard my mum say, 'It would be so lovely, wouldn't it?' and then Dad said, 'Gary would be thrilled. It's not really much fun being an only child, is it?'"

"Then what did your mum say?" Robert asked.

"Her voice went all sort of soppy and she said, 'A little baby, wouldn't it be wonderful.' Then I couldn't listen any more 'cause I'd throw up."

His mum and dad were back together again and that's what he'd wanted, at least that's what he thought. At first it was great but ... Gary was used to living with his mum, just his mum. He'd forgotten – Dad seemed to take up so much space and in the morning, he took ages in the bathroom and there was only one toilet in the house. Still, it was handy when they were going to a City game, and for quite a few other things, too. But now all this talk of a baby...

"Do you know what, Gary?" Robert's gran said, confidently. "You have absolutely nothing to worry about. Sure, your mum and dad have no intention of having another baby – they're too old, for one thing. Arrah, babies are nothing but trouble. Now why would they bother with a baby at their stage of life when they have everything sorted out?"

"But they said so, I *heard* them—" Gary started.

"Take no notice of that, Gary. You probably heard wrong. I'll bet you anything you like, your mum and dad won't have another baby."

"Are you sure, Gran?" Robert asked.

"Almost definitely! Sometimes people get funny notions about babies but when they see the trouble they cause, they soon go off the idea. Don't worry, Gary – there won't be any more babies in your house."

But there was still an itching doubt in Gary's mind.

"By the way, Gary. What did Mr Doyle say when you asked him?" Robert's gran asked, her eyes twinkling with fun. This time Robert told his gran the story.

They had asked to stay behind to have a quiet word with their teacher. "How do you stop people having babies?" Robert had asked him straight out.

"How do you stop people having babies?" Mr Doyle repeated the question slowly as if he was working out the answer in his brain. "Is this a trick question?" He looked suspiciously at Gary and Robert.

"No, honest sir. We know someone who's thinking about having another baby and we just want to show them it would be a *big* mistake," Robert said.

"Oh," Mr Doyle said, looking relieved. "I know a really good way – ask them to spend half a day in our classroom. It would put them off children for life!"

"Be serious, sir!" Robert said.

"I am serious, Robert," Mr Doyle said, smiling. "But you know, if there were no more babies, I'd be out of a job in ten years' time."

"You could always become a groundsman for City," Gary suggested.

"Or sell programmes?" Mr Doyle added. "So – who is this person ... the one you want to stop having babies?"

"Just someone ... we know," Gary said, avoiding Mr Doyle's gaze.

"Anyone I know?" he asked.

"No," said Gary, quickly.

Mr Doyle didn't say any more, neither did Gary or Robert. It was obvious that Mr Doyle knew a good deal about most things but he knew absolutely *nothing* about having babies.

Gran smiled as Robert spoke about the conversation with his teacher. "Well, fair play to Mr Doyle – he has a point. If everyone stopped having babies, there would be no children in the schools and then no schools," Gran said.

"Excellent!" Robert cheered.

"I'm not bothered about anyone else," Gary said, forcefully. "I just don't want any babies in *our* house!"

FOUR

Babies were not the only thing troubling Gary. The million pound legs of City's most expensive signing, Tyrone Bradley, were finding it hard to run from one end of the field to the other. (Gary and Robert used to call it the pitch, but now Gary Lineker, on *Football Focus*, called it 'the field', even though it wasn't a field. You don't see many fields as green and neat as that!)

City's supporters grumbled quietly as they walked home. Their team had lost to four easy goals from a poor opposition. "What is wrong with Tyrone Bradley?" they asked, as one voice. "After all the money we've spent on him ... he does nothing, he's useless!"

"A donkey could do better!"

"We should have bought a donkey from Blackpool beach!"

It was true, Tyrone Bradley was like a donkey on a wet day at the seaside. He was useless. City should get rid of him, Gary thought. But Gary had his reasons, other reasons for thinking like that. Every time he saw Tyrone Bradley, Gary was reminded of the letters that he and Robert had written to him, trying to arrange a meeting with his mum. It had been so embarrassing – that's why Gary wanted City to sell Tyrone Bradley to another club and use the money to buy a better striker.

"Bottom of the table again," Eugene McNab said. "It's depressing isn't it, son?"

It was too painful for Gary and Robert. On Saturday evening Gary felt as if he wanted to cry, *really* cry. It was awful seeing City lose – it hurt watching the other side score four easy goals.

"The lad's in a bad way," Mr Doyle said on Monday morning, two days after City had lost four–nil at home. It was a wet and windy morning. Gary and Robert had walked to school battling against the rain, with a gale blowing into their faces, stinging their noses. Mr Doyle watched them as they crossed the playground and fought with the door into school.

"Can you give us a hand, lads?" he asked, even before they had time to wipe the weather from their faces. Mr Doyle was struggling with a pile of display boards. "We need to put these up near the main entrance."

Gary and Robert slung their bags into the far corner of the cloakroom and helped Mr Doyle carry the boards through the school.

"What are these for, sir?" Robert asked.

"For a display," Mr Doyle said.

"What sort of display?" Robert probed.

"A surprise," Mr Doyle said in a vague tone. Then he changed the subject with a litany of complaints about City in general, Tyrone Bradley in particular.

Later, after registration, when the room was steaming with wet clothes drying on ancient radiators, Mr Doyle said, "Listen, everyone, I have a surprise for you." The way he announced it made the whole class stop talking and look up. Mr Doyle walked out of the classroom. He was gone for several minutes. The class began to take advantage of his absence, moving around, chatting and shouting. A few minutes later, he walked back in again wearing different clothes and carrying a small, long, black case. He didn't seem at all annoyed with the level of noise in the class.

"That was clever, sir!" Robert called. Gary started to giggle nervously. What was going on?

"Good morning, children," Mr Doyle said. Only it wasn't *quite* Mr Doyle's voice. It was a softer tone – and his smile was slightly different, too.

"Good morning Mr Doyle," the children replied, confused, they'd already said good morning earlier on. Now they were curious... Suddenly, the real Mr Doyle walked back into the room. Laughing heartily, he shook the other man's hand.

"Children, I'd like to introduce my brother, Colum Doyle. Father Colum Doyle!"

"Are you twins?" Kieran Sackville shouted.

"Manners, Kieran," Mr Doyle chided. "Yes, we're twins."

"Identical?" Kieran added.

"What do you think?" Mr Doyle asked. The whole class giggled nervously. Yes, they were identical. Gary couldn't stop looking at their faces, apart from a slight tan on Father Colum's face, he was *exactly* like Mr Doyle. They even had the same glasses.

"Sir, my mum's doing a special study on twins," Gary said. His mum was a midwife at the local hospital. Mr Doyle shuffled uneasily at the mention of Gary's mum's name.

"Good," he said, clearing his throat. The class rippled with excitement as the two Doyles stood, watching the children examine their faces for differences. "Now then, class, I want you to be very, very quiet and listen," Mr Doyle said, in a serious voice. "My twin, Father Colum, is going to be with us for a fortnight and in that time he's going to help all of us. So I want you to be good and listen."

"Good morning again," Father Colum said. He lifted the black case on to the desk and began to open it. "Do you know what's in here?" he asked. The class shuffled and muttered but no one raised their hands. "Go on, have a guess," he said.

"Your sandwiches!" Robert shouted. The class giggled.

"No," Father Colum replied pleasantly. "Good guess, though."

"Your work things?" Kieran suggested.

"You're getting warmer," Father Colum said,

creaking open the black case a little more.

"Your gear for changing into?" Tessie Morgan volunteered.

"Do you mean, like a football kit?" Father Colum teased. The class laughed. Tessie blushed.

"No. The stuff you wear for church services," Tessie added, a little annoyed.

"Another very good guess. Any other ideas?"

The class was silent, waiting for the truth to emerge. Father Colum creaked the case completely open and then lifted out – a mandolin. The class were unimpressed – they'd expected something much more exciting. Father Colum crashed his hands against the strings making a painful racket. "That's what this sounds like. Lovely, isn't it?" Father Colum asked.

"No!" the children replied, encouraged by Mr Doyle.

"Are you sure?" Father Colum asked, twanging the instrument again.

"Yes!" the class protested.

"There's a story about this instrument. Shall I tell you?"

"OK," a few children muttered.

"I found this mandolin," Father Colum

explained. "In our attic at home. It was left in a corner, covered in dust and cobwebs. I wasn't sure what it was so I brought it downstairs and tried to play it, just like I did a minute ago but it was broken. Well, at least I *thought* it was broken. I felt quite sad about it but anyway, I polished it and stood it in the corner of my sitting room because it looked nice – the beautiful varnished wood and the shiny strings. I thought it made a lovely ornament. It does look nice, doesn't it?" Father Colum asked.

"Yes," the class responded.

"I polished and polished the mandolin and it stood in the corner of my room for about three years. Then, one day, a stranger came to visit me. He looked at the mandolin in the corner of the room and said, 'What a beautiful instrument. Is it all right for me to pick it up?' I said it was and he stroked the wood like a mother caressing her baby."

The class were totally silent, spellbound as Father Colum told his story. They watched in fascination as he stroked the polished wood of the mandolin.

"Then the stranger said, 'Do you mind if I play your mandolin?' I told him that it was broken, that I'd tried to play it but it had probably been too many years in the attic. Even so, the stranger began to twist the pegs of the mandolin, just like this," Father Colum adjusted the strings. "Then he plucked at the strings until the mandolin was eventually in tune. 'Do you mind if I play a tune?' the stranger asked. I said he could try. So he did and it sounded like this."

Father Colum began to play the mandolin. At first, the children were a little embarrassed. Then, as he plucked his way through a beautiful melody, the whole class sat amazed and entranced. It seemed as though he played for ages. Gary gazed out of the window and watched as the clouds danced to the rhythm of the music.

When Father Colum stopped playing, it felt as though the class were sitting in a different room. "Now, would you like to sing?" he asked.

"Yes, good idea," Tessie said.

"No!" the boys chorused. "We don't like singing. Play some more."

"Do you mind if I ask you something," Gary said. "How did you learn to play?"

"Well, after the stranger went home that day, I began fiddling about with the old mandolin and I did that every day until I got a little tune. I suppose I taught myself."

"But the stranger started you off," Tessie suggested.

"That's very, very true," Father Colum agreed, nodding his head. "I feel a bit like the stranger today, coming in here, talking about my mandolin," Father Colum said. "Let's have a song now. The words to this are very simple. I'll sing them first and then you repeat after me..."

Within a few minutes, the reluctant singers were belting out a new song and clapping their hands to the beat. They repeated the easy verse over and over again until they were confident about the words and the tune.

Father Colum stopped playing but gestured to the class to continue singing for one more verse. Then he held up his hands for them to stop. "Brilliant! Fantastic!" he enthused. "Just like my mandolin – when you're tuned up and polished and handled carefully, you can all sing like angels."

The class giggled, shuffled and smiled – twenty-eight potential angels, waiting for the next tune to begin. "You know, children," Father Colum said, "if you want to, you can do anything."

Gary and Robert shuffled excitedly in their seats. Things were going to be really good with Father Colum in school.

FIVE

Robert was sitting and staring at his coat on the washing line. He pressed his nose against the window to get a better view. The water was dripping steadily from the bottom of his coat.

The doorbell rang.

"Robert! It's Gary," Robert's mum shouted.

Gary wandered upstairs to Robert's room. "You coming out? On the bikes?" he asked.

"Can't," Robert said. "Mum's washed my coat."

"What for?"

"Me and Kieran were playing rugby on the field on the way home—" Robert began.

"Is that why your mum's in a bad mood?" Gary asked.

"Yes, probably..." Robert said, his voice drifting away.

"Why don't you put your coat in the tumble dryer?" Gary suggested.

"It's dripping wet," Robert sighed.

"Won't do it any harm – I sometimes do that," Gary said, encouraging Robert.

The two boys crept downstairs and through the kitchen, out into the back garden.

"Hey, I didn't know you had a new goal net," Gary said, as he ran up the garden towards the washing line.

"Gran bought it for me yesterday at a car boot sale. She was selling cakes," Robert replied.

"Can I have a go?" Gary asked. "You go in goal, I'll be Tyrone Bradley. We can practise taking penalties..."

"No, I'm not meant to be out," Robert protested.

"Your mum won't see you, she's in the front room," Gary said.

"She might if she comes out to make a cup of —"

"She won't!" Gary insisted.

Robert quickly took his dripping coat from the line and placed it inside the new goal net, just like a professional goalie. He rubbed his hands together and then opened them out, ready for action.

"I don't believe it!" Gary said, in the voice of a television commentator. "The ref has blown for a penalty! The United players are surrounding the ref, protesting about his decision. Tyrone Bradley confidently steps up to the spot..." Gary walked a few paces back from the goal.

"The United goalie is ready for anything," Robert said, continuing the commentary. "He watches carefully as Bradley prepares to take the most important penalty kick of his career."

Gary ran forward and blasted the ball into the top corner of the net. Robert dived to stop the ball but caught his foot in the loose netting of the goal, pulling the whole structure to the ground, on top of his wet coat. He lay underneath the netting, giggling at his misfortune.

Gary cartwheeled around the garden celebrating his penalty goal. "Look at Bradley!" he continued in his commentator's voice. "The relief and joy in his acrobatics as he jumps and leaps around the field!"

Robert crawled from under the collapsed net and dragged out his dripping, dirty coat. "Oh no! My coat's covered in mud *again*!"

"Shall we put the net back up and have a few

more goes, Robert?" Gary asked, ignoring Robert's moans. "It's brilliant having your own net in the garden."

"Look at my coat!"

"Just leave it there, we'll sort it out later," Gary insisted, as he lifted the goal back into place.

After a few moments staring at his wet coat, Robert hurled it into the back of the net and the boys took turns at being Tyrone Bradley or the United goalie. They dived, rolled and performed elaborate cartwheels whenever the ball went over the line and into the back of the net. The dripping coat was completely forgotten.

The score was seven–all. "Let's do a sudden death," Gary suggested.

"Good idea," Robert agreed. "I'll go first." He stepped back to take the vital kick, but then they were interrupted.

"Robert! Robert!" Robert's mum was at the kitchen window banging and shouting. "Come here! Where's your coat?"

Robert and Gary dragged the soggy, filthy coat back into the kitchen. "Look at the state of you two. What have you been doing?"

"Shooting!" Gary replied.

"Penalty shoot outs – with my new goalie net," Robert added.

"You're filthy!" Mum exclaimed.

"We were just going to do a sudden death..." Gary explained.

"And look at your coat, Robert – it's disgusting. What have you been doing with it, rolling in the mud?"

"Gary said we could put it in the tumble drier. Then it'll be dry," Robert said. "We were just bringing it in."

"What?" Robert's mum asked, her eyes wide with disbelief. "Is that what you do in your house, Gary?"

"Yes, sometimes," Gary said, hesitantly. "I'd better go – I'll see you tomorrow, Robert." He ran back through the house without another word.

"And you'd better get an early bath, son," Robert's mum said, a little less annoyed. "And *don't* forget to wash your face!"

The next morning, Robert and Gary listened as Father Colum told them another story. He was a great storyteller and it was brilliant just listening to him. Then he started to talk about something else.

"This week I want you to think about prayer – about talking to God – and I would like you to pray for just one special thing. You know, God isn't like Santa Claus, he won't deliver bikes or CD players on December 25th. Pray about something which might be making you feel sad or unhappy. Pray for anything, but make it just one special thing – only one thing." The class listened intently to Father Colum's words. "Prayer can be like a postcard or a telephone call. If it's a postcard, it's just a short message like the sort you send home from holidays. If it's a letter, it will be longer and more detailed. A telephone call can be more personal and chatty..."

Gary's mind wandered off and he stopped listening to the gentle tones of Father Colum. There were two important things on his mind and he wanted answers to both of them.

1 *He wanted Mum and Dad to stop thinking about, and to stop talking about having another baby. Babies were messy and noisy and expensive and nothing but trouble*

2 *He wanted City to start playing properly again so that they could move out of the relegation zone.*

He wanted Tyrone Bradley, City's million pound signing, to start scoring goals again. He had been absolutely pathetic this season. Even more than that, he wanted Tyrone Bradley to be transferred to another club. He was an embarrassment

As Gary's mind focused on Tyrone Bradley's poor form, a clean piece of paper appeared on his desk and he tuned into what Father Colum was saying again.

"Remember, I only want you to write one thing down on this piece of paper. Not a list, just choose one thing, but you can write it as a postcard, a letter or a telephone call."

"What shall I choose?" Gary asked himself. "Babies or City?"

"Then we'll put your prayer requests in a box and have a very special service. Maybe at that service, you would like to read out your special request..."

"I can't pray for no babies," Gary thought. "Everyone would laugh at me reading that out."

So Gary wrote his prayer:

This is a postcard prayer

Dear God, I hope you're well. I know I haven't been praying much lately. I've had a lot of things on my mind. I want to ask you to help Tyrone Bradley to score lots of goals so that City will move up the table and out of the danger zone and if you think it's the right thing, I would like Tyrone Bradley to be transferred. He might be happier at another club. Amen.

Later, Gary and Robert compared notes. "What did you write?" Robert asked.

"I wrote about City," Gary replied.

"What about your mum and dad and the babies?" Robert asked again.

"I don't know. I didn't think it was as important as City. Your gran said they were too old..."

"I prayed for my mum to cheer up," Robert said.

"Do you think God will answer our prayers?" Gary asked.

"Probably," Robert replied. "Mr Doyle's brother seems to know what he's talking about."

SIX

There was something about Father Colum and
something very different about school just now. So
much so that Gary had absolutely no problems
jumping out of bed the following morning. It was as
though Father Colum understood what the children
were going through, what really worried them and
so school was suddenly better, sweeter, and life was
a whole lot easier.

"Mum will be surprised," Gary thought as he
washed and dressed quickly. Normally, she had to
call him hundreds of times and sometimes she even
had to drag him from his bed.

She was surprised. She looked quite shocked, so
did Dad, when Gary bounded into the room with a,

"Duh dah..." like a circus performer. Gary's face fell as he saw Mum and Dad sitting at the far end of the table, looking cosy and reading a leaflet together.

Gary slumped into a chair a mile away from Mum and Dad. He felt suddenly sort of cold and alone and just for a moment, he wished that he was unwell so that his mum would make a fuss of him.

"Gary," Dad said, sensing that something was not quite right. "Come and sit down next to your old dad. I want to talk to you about something..."

"What are you reading, Dad?" Gary asked, moving to sit closer to him.

"I'll get your breakfast, Gary," Mum volunteered.

"Oh this? Oh ... it's nothing," he said, flicking it to one side. Gary tried to pick it up. "Well, actually it's something your mum collected from the hospital..."

"It's not about babies is it?" Gary asked, with a groan.

Dad looked embarrassed. "Well, actually it is. How did you guess?"

"Probably the picture of the baby on the front?" Gary said, trying to sound sarcastic.

Mum placed the cereal and toast in front of Gary. "We think it would be really good for you to have a brother or sister," Mum said. "But we know that it won't be easy for you, Gary. That's what this leaflet is about."

"I *hate* babies," Gary said, almost in a whisper.

"That's what all boys say, isn't it, son?" Dad said.

"How do you know you hate them? You haven't really had much chance to experience a baby," Mum said, trying to soothe Gary.

"And they're not babies for ever. When it's bigger, you'll be able to play football with him and you'll be great mates when you grow up," Dad said, reassuringly. "It's not all dirty nappies and screaming fits, you know."

"But what if it's a girl?" groaned Gary.

"It doesn't make any difference, Gary," Mum said. "Girls are people too."

"No they're not. They whine and tell tales and play with stupid toys and they're pathetic at football. That is my *worst* nightmare – to have a sister!" Mum and Dad just stared at Gary as he spoke.

"And if you have a baby you'll spend all our money on it and there'll be nothing left for me, so what will happen when I need new trainers or football boots?" Gary said, pushing his cereal away.

"We'll still buy whatever you need, Gary – it's not going to make any difference to the way we treat you..." Mum said, trying to reason with Gary.

"Yes it will. There'll be no money left for me!"

"Eat your breakfast, Gary," Mum said gently.

"I'm not hungry."

"You'll be hungry when you get to school, son," Dad said.

"We haven't talked about all the lovely positive things about having another member of the family, like—" Mum began.

"Dirty nappies and screaming babies and never having any sleep at night," Gary said in between mouthfuls.

"It would be lovely to have a baby, absolutely wonderful," Mum said, ignoring Gary's negative comments. "Anyway, who's filled your head with all this nonsense about them?"

"Tessie at school. She's told me. They had a new baby and she says it's hell in her house!"

"Yes, but..." Dad sighed as he began to speak.

"And we saw that film, remember it, Mum? About the baby who was so dreadful that the mum and dad left home and gave it to their ten-year-old daughter to look after. What a nightmare!" Gary said, getting carried away with his horror stories.

"Gary, what you need to realise is—" Dad began.

"Eugene, I think it's best if we leave it for now," Mum said, leaning on the back of Gary's chair, making faces at Dad as if to say, "There's no point arguing about it."

"Why don't we get a dog, instead?" Gary suggested.

"Because..." Dad started.

"Come on, it's time we were all heading off for the day," Mum said.

"What's wrong with a dog, Mum?" Gary asked.

"We've had this discussion before, Gary. We're not at home all day, so it wouldn't be fair to a dog," she said, slightly annoyed.

"But it won't be fair to leave a baby at home all day by itself, either!" Gary said.

"We won't leave the baby at home. I'll give up work for a—" Mum began.

"See, I'm right! Then there won't be any money for anything!" Gary interrupted.

"It doesn't work like that, Gary. You'll still be able to have your trainers and football boots—" Dad began.

"And, I'm not sharing my bedroom with anyone!

And I'm not sharing my things!" Gary shouted.

"Calm down, Gary," Mum said. "I don't understand why you're being like this. If your dad and I had been so selfish when we were first married, we would never have had you. You wouldn't exist!"

"That was different!" Gary hissed. Mum cleared the breakfast bowls and walked out of the room sighing and shaking her head.

"Tell you what, Gary," Dad said, "This evening, when you're a bit calmer..."

"I am calm," Gary snapped.

"Yes, yes. This evening when we're all a lot calmer, why don't you sit down quietly and write a list of all the reasons why you don't want a new brother or sister. Will you do that for me?"

"OK," Gary agreed reluctantly. "I'll write a list and I'll show you!"

"And tomorrow, there's a cracking game coming up. When City win, we can all forget about babies. What do you say, Gary?"

"Right!" Gary hit his father's hand and then realised the challenge before him. He would need more than God on his side. Robert would have to help, too.

SEVEN

Robert said he'd help Gary to compile the list. Gary told him it was urgent, so, the next evening, they did it straight after school at Robert's house – away from prying eyes.

This is Why I Don't Want A Baby
by Gary

1 A baby would scream all night and keep me awake so all I could do in the day would be sleep and my school work would suffer and I would become thick and it would be all the fault of the new baby

48

2 *New babies cost a lot of money. There might not be any money left for important things like going to see City or new trainers, or holidays. There might not even be enough money for food for ourselves*

3 *Mum would have to stop work so there would be even less money. Then she would probably be unhappy because I know that she loves her work. Then all the ladies on her ward would be unhappy – just because of one little baby*

4 *Babies take up too much space and we haven't got enough space in our house anyway. They have to have lots of stuff like prams and cots and car seats. (More money)*

5 *When they're very little, babies are sick a lot and they leave a mess all over the place – not just on the furniture, on the floor, on clothes – probably on my lovely new track suit, too*

6 *Babies' nappies are really disgusting and stink and when they need changing they smell so bad that it almost makes me throw up*

7 Even if we could go on holiday, we'd have to buy a bigger car for the baby's pram and we can't afford a better car now, so we definitely wouldn't be able to afford one if a baby came along, and that means we definitely wouldn't be able to go on holiday

8 I would have to push the pram round the streets while I was looking after my new baby brother. This is not a cool thing to do. How can I play football in the park with a pram? (And don't say that I could use it for a goal post because if the ball hit the pram or the baby, I would be in deep trouble)

9 If you're just having a baby so that I can have a brother or sister, don't bother because I don't need one! I've got Robert and loads of friends and that's all I need

Robert was getting impatient making the list. "I think that's enough, Gary. That should put them off."

"No, it can't be. You can't have nine things in a list!" Gary protested.

"Why not?"

"Because it's an uneven number, it's bad luck," Gary explained.

"Who says?"

Gary searched for a reply. "It's common knowledge. You always make your lists even numbers – like the ten commandments. There weren't eleven or nine."

"Let's cross one off, then," Robert suggested.

"No, let's add another one. There aren't eight commandments," Gary said.

"I can't think of any more and it'll soon be time for tea and then we're going to the match," Robert whined.

"We'll just *have* to think of another one," Gary said, desperately. "They won't take it seriously if there are only nine things."

"I've just thought of one!" Robert said, triumphantly. He wrote it down.

10 *If you have a baby and you realise you don't like it, you can't send it back. It isn't like a toy doll. You have to keep it for ever, like a puppy. (But with puppies you can even give them to another owner. You can't do that with a baby.) That's why I don't think this is a good idea*

"Great! Where shall we leave it?" Gary asked. "On top of your television. They'll definitely see it there, under the remote control. But wait until after the football."

"Good idea, Robert. This will do the trick! This will put them off babies for life!"

When they first set off for the football ground, Robert, Gary and Gary's dad had the pavement to themselves. They talked about school and football – Dad chipping in every few minutes asking boring questions like, "Do you enjoy Maths, Robert?" As if anyone would actually *enjoy* Maths.

At every junction the pavement became more and more crowded and soon Robert, Gary and his dad were surrounded by enthusiastic City fans, en route to the match. No more silly talk about school now – the crowd marched as one, and weaved in and out of shared conversations. "High hopes tonight," one man said, as he passed Gary's group.

"City have got to win," Gary's dad agreed.

"Tyrone Bradley badly needs to score!" Robert remarked.

Inside the stadium, Gary sat in silence and stared at

the thousands of fans who were filing down the stands into their seats. He had high hopes, really high hopes for tonight's match. He hoped, prayed, that tonight he wouldn't be disappointed. But he'd been here before – the excitement and hopefulness before City played. He was always optimistic before every match but he knew the taste of disappointment. "Please God, please God, let them win tonight," he whispered.

"What are you thinking?" Gary's dad asked.

"I'm praying for City to win," Gary admitted.

"What?" Robert asked, his face creased with disbelief.

"Like Father Colum said – if you want something badly, ask God for it. So, I'm asking God for a win for City," Gary said, his voice lowered so that the other cynical fans couldn't hear him. "I'm doing a telephone call sort of prayer. Remember ... 'Hello God, just ringing to ask you something'."

"Father Colum said you can't ask for things like this or a bike or a CD player. God isn't like Santa Claus," Robert reminded his friend.

"I'm not asking for a bike," Gary argued. "Just for City to win."

"Now they'll probably lose, Gary. God will show

you that you're not supposed to ask for things like that," Robert said. "Not even if you phone him!"

"I don't think God works like that, Robert. I'm sure he doesn't do things out of spite," Gary's dad said.

"I bet we lose, Gary, and if we do, it's all your fault!" said Robert.

"They'll win, you watch..." and the rest of Gary's words were drowned by the noise of the teams emerging from the tunnel and spilling out on to the pitch.

The cheers and the chants were deafening as City warmed up and kicked six balls around the field. The greatest chant of all came from the kop end of the ground. "Tyrone Bradley, we love you badly, Tyrone Bradley we need you badly, Tyrone Bradley we need you badly, oh ... Tyrone we love you."

The noise and excitement in the stadium reached boiling point when the referee blew his whistle for the start of the match. The City players kicked the ball about confidently and immediately started putting the pressure on the visiting team. Surprisingly, within minutes the fans were dancing and cheering in their seats as Tyrone Bradley had scored. He had headed an impossible cross into the back of the net. One–nil!

"Yesss!" Gary and Robert shrieked and then hugged each other. Gary's dad jumped up as if he had been stung in the foot. "The famine is over, Tyrone has scored!" he shouted.

By the time the referee blew the whistle for half-time, Tyrone Bradley had scored another goal – now City were winning by two goals to nil. "Let's celebrate with a pie and a cuppa," Gary's dad suggested.

Even though he didn't like pies, Robert agreed and the three made their way to the famous City Pie Stall. They were really surprised when they saw Father Colum entertaining the pie queue with his mandolin. He was accompanied by someone playing an accordion and another person playing a flute. Gary thought they sounded beautiful. Mr Doyle was watching as they played and sang. Father Colum spotted the boys. "How are you doing, lads?" he called, in the middle of a song.

"Brilliant!" Robert said. "Aren't City fantastic tonight?"

"Excellent," Mr Doyle said, replying for his brother who was coming to the end of a song.

"They're raising money for the Special Baby Unit," he explained.

"Are you enjoying the match?" Gary's dad asked the two men, putting some money into the tin next to Father Colum's mandolin.

"We are indeed – and what a bonus, meeting these two – a regular partnership!" Father Colum said brightly. "What do you think of the music?"

"It's good," Gary said, uncertainly. He didn't like the idea of collecting money for babies.

"Looks like Tyrone Bradley has rediscovered his legs, eh lads?" Mr Doyle said, winking at Gary and Robert, interrupting Gary's thoughts.

Later, as they watched a boring second half, Gary gazed over the stand and the local buildings to a starlit sky. "Robert, if we win, that means my prayer has been answered," he said, almost as if he was on another planet.

"No it doesn't," Robert said. "I can't see God reaching his hand down on to the pitch and putting Tyrone in the right places to score!"

"Do you mean like Subbuteo?" Gary asked.

"Yes! God picks Tyrone up by the scruff of his shorts and puts him in front of the goal mouth..."

"You're right, Robert," Gary's dad agreed.

"God's not like that. He probably helped Tyrone get fit and gave him his confidence back. Then he made the other team tired or something," Gary insisted.

"City have played well for a change, that's all," Dad said.

Gary didn't believe them. He had suddenly got religion – in a *big* way. And, if God could answer *this* prayer, there was an even bigger prayer that Gary needed answering. It was to do with babies.

EIGHT

Gary went to bed in a brilliant mood but his sleep was disturbed by a dream, a nightmare. It was a bad nightmare. Hundreds of babies were crawling around his room, all over his bed and cupboards. They were pulling the City posters off the wall and jumping on to the computer keyboard until smoke began to billow out of the visual display unit. Gary felt paralysed, he shouted at the babies to get out of his room, but they just giggled and gurgled at him.

One baby, in a blue babygro, climbed on to Gary's stomach and bounced up and down as if Gary was a mattress or a trampoline. "Get off!" Gary shouted but still the baby jumped on him. It seemed as though its foot would go right through him at any minute. He felt a pain, a terrible pain. He watched helplessly as the physio stood at the side of his room waiting to run on to help him. There was no sign of the referee, so Gary lay helpless, longing for the physio to come over.

"Help!" he screamed. "Help! Get this thing off me!"

When he woke, his mum and dad were standing by the side of his bed, and Mum had her cool hand on his forehead.

"What's wrong?" Dad was asking him. "Have you had a bad dream?"

"My stomach," Gary murmured, "...my stomach. It's been injured."

"What?" Mum whispered.

"There were lots of babies ... one on my stomach ... and some on the computer and ... up the walls and ... they wouldn't go. I shouted at them. They were horrible, really frightening..."

"You've had a bad dream," Mum soothed.

"But my stomach hurts where it was sitting on me," Gary insisted.

"Who?" Dad asked.

"The baby. The blue baby. It was horrible. Horrible. My stomach hurts," Gary groaned.

"Must have been something you ate," Mum said. "You didn't have a pie, did you?"

"What?" Dad asked.

"At the football. You didn't have one of their awful pies, did you?" Mum asked again.

"Ye-es," Dad admitted, like a guilty child.

"Those pies always make Gary ill. Why did you buy one?" said Mum again, interrogating Dad at four o'clock in the morning. Gary pulled the duvet over his head and tried to go back to sleep.

"We were celebrating," Dad said, meekly.

"Celebrating what?" Mum said, getting angry.

"Tyrone Bradley scoring a goal." Dad spoke with such uncertainty that it was impossible to tell if he had been dreaming. "He's fine now, love. Look, he's asleep."

Bernadette kissed the duvet where Gary's head might have been. "You'll be fine in the morning," she whispered.

"Fingers crossed," Dad added.

"Please God," Gary sighed. His stomach still hurt, but not as much as the memory of that dreadful dream.

"It's all this talk about babies as well," Mum whispered, sympathetically. "I never realised he hated the idea so much."

Under the bedclothes, Gary grinned triumphantly. "At last! She's beginning to understand," he thought.

The dreadful dream replayed on the video inside his head as Gary walked to school next morning. Robert looked a bit delicate, as well, as he waited for Gary outside the school gates.

"Are you sick, too?" Robert asked.

"Yeah – and I've had a terrible dream," Gary said. "My mum says those pies are full of salmonella."

"They're not. They've just got funny meat in them," Robert replied. Gary looked to see if he was joking but he wasn't. "What was your dream about?"

"Babies!" Gary said.

"Ugh! What a nightmare," said Robert.

"It's frightening what they can do, Robert," Gary said, seriously. "We've just got to keep reminding my mum and dad about the danger of babies!"

"You're right," Robert agreed.

"And praying. Father Colum said, when you're in a storm start praying but don't stop rowing," Gary said, wisely. "We can do it, Robert!"

"How though?" Robert asked.

"We've got to keep the pressure on my mum and dad," Gary said. "I think they're having second thoughts already. I heard them talking about our list in the middle of the night."

"Excellent!" Robert said.

"Yes," Gary said, confidently, "We can definitely do it."

"We need a proper plan. You know, to keep up the pressure," Robert suggested.

"Like what?" Gary asked.

"Well, maybe we've got to do something..." Robert searched for words, "...more obvious!"

"Such as?"

"Like show your mum and dad that babies really are a big nuisance and dead irritating," Robert said.

"So how do we do that?" Gary enquired.

"We'll have to think about it," Robert said. "We need to have a really good plan." The truth was, Robert had very little idea what to do. He only knew that he really wanted to help his friend and he loved making plans and seeing things happen.

Then something did happen.

Mr Doyle was collecting the Maths homework after

break. There were one or two notes handed in instead of homework and then Tessie said, "Our baby's teething, sir, and he was screaming all evening. We couldn't even watch the TV properly, it was that bad. I haven't done my homework and my mum couldn't write a note because she's so busy with the baby and she said if you don't believe me, you've got to ring and you'll see for yourself how much noise our baby makes."

"You mean, 'hear' for myself," Mr Doyle said.

"What, sir?" Tessie asked, irritated by Mr Doyle's correction.

"If I ring your mum I won't 'see' for myself. I'll 'hear' for myself."

"You can if you want but I wouldn't if I was you," Tessie said.

Father Colum laughed heartily at Tessie's correction. Then, in a serious tone he said, "I think your mum could do with some help, don't you, Tessie?"

"You're right, Father," Robert said. "Tessie needs help, too, and I think I know a way that we can help – me and Gary."

"Do you?" Gary asked, not quite sure of Robert's thoughts.

"Yes," Robert said, his eyes twinkling.

"Help *Tessie*?" Gary hissed. "Are you ill, Robert?"

"Good lads," Father Colum said as the two boys were about to leave the classroom at the end of the day.

"Thanks, Father," Robert replied.

"You two boys always seem to be planning – sure, you're a couple of holy terrors – I'm certain you could think of a way to help Tessie. Perhaps you could invite her round for tea or something?" Father Colum suggested.

"Yes, I had thought of that," Robert said. Gary's eyes grew round in amazement.

"I wouldn't say Tessie gets many invites to tea," Father Colum said, quietly.

"She doesn't, Father," Gary said.

"That's a shame. She's such a lovely girl," he said.

"Yes, she is nice," said Robert. "For a girl."

Gary was totally puzzled. "What are you up to?" he asked as they left school.

"Wait and see," Robert whispered.

They caught up with Tessie just outside the school gates. "Hi, Tessie. Are you all right?" Robert shouted.

"What's up with you?" Tessie asked suspiciously.

"We've been thinking. Me and Gary—"

"Makes a change," she said.

"D'you want to come round to tea one evening?" Robert asked.

"*What?*" Tessie asked, disbelieving.

"Would you like to come round for tea?" Robert repeated the question.

"What for?" Tessie said, in a hostile voice.

Robert hadn't thought it would be this hard. "Me and Gary would like to help you ... with your baby sister."

"Why? What's the catch? Nobody ever invites me round for tea," Tessie said. "Anyway – it's a boy, a brother."

"Your baby brother, then. After what Father Colum said today, me and Gary were thinking we'd like to help you. So d'you want to come to tea, or not?"

"Is this a trick?" Tessie asked.

"No. Honest. We're just trying to help," Robert replied. "Gary's mum is brilliant with babies, you can get her advice."

"My mum?" Gary squealed. Robert shoved him to stop him saying any more.

"OK, I'll come but I'll have to bring the baby with me or my mum won't let me go. I have to look after him after school," Tessie said.

"We'll see you tomorrow then," Robert said.

"Don't tell anyone in school. They might get the wrong idea," Tessie said, cautiously. "Where do you live?"

"Thirty-two Ramsey Grove," Robert said.

"That's my house!" Gary protested.

"Yes, Gary," Robert said gently. "And that's where we're all having tea – Tessie, her baby brother, you, me and your mum, who loves babies."

"It better not be a trick," Tessie shouted as she ran off.

"Why is Tessie coming to my house?" Gary asked.

"Because we want your mum to meet a squealing baby. Now ... what time does your mum get home from work, normally?" Robert asked his friend.

"About twenty to six," Gary replied, automatically. He still wasn't sure what was going on.

"Good. Then we'll get Tessie to arrive at a quarter to six."

"She won't be happy if people arrive when she's just home from work," Gary said.

"Why not?" Robert asked.

"Because she likes a bit of peace and quiet for a few minutes. She likes to kick off her shoes and have five minutes' peace..."

"Exactly!"

"What?" Gary was lost with Robert's plan.

"If Tessie comes in with the screaming baby just when your mum needs a break, then she'll know what babies are like."

"She might be cross with me for inviting Tessie," Gary said, thinking aloud. "Even though I didn't invite her, you did!"

"She won't, you'll see," Robert said, confidently. "But if she is, that's all part of our excellent plan!"

NINE

Tessie arrived just after quarter to six, as planned. Before she came in, she looked all around her to check that nobody could actually see her going into Gary's house. "I have to bring the pram inside," she announced. "Just in case – it might get nicked."

"Who's this?" Mum asked. She had only just got home.

"Tessie," Gary said.

"Who's Tessie?" Mum asked again.

"She's in our class at school."

"Gary, why is she here, with that baby?" Mum whispered. "You know I like a little break when I get in from work."

Tessie's baby brother's screaming filled the whole

house. "Sorry, Mrs McNab," Tessie said. "He's always crying like this. Oh, thanks for inviting me for tea."

"For tea?" Mum said, looking at Gary. Gary shrugged his shoulders as if it was nothing to do with him. "What's wrong with your baby?" Mum asked.

"Teething," Tessie said. "He keeps us awake – all of us, all night. My mum says she feels like handing him back to the hospital. It's doing her head in."

"Your poor mum. She must be having a really hard time," Bernadette said, softening towards Tessie. "Do you mind if I hold him for a minute?" Bernadette asked. Gary and Robert looked at one another, panic-stricken. This wasn't part of the plan. She lifted the baby carefully out of the pram and held him snugly on her shoulder. "What's his name, Tessie?"

"Norton. He's called Norton," Tessie said flatly.

"Norton?" Gary snorted. He had only ever heard it called, 'the baby'.

"That's an unusual name," Gary's mum said in a sing-song voice as she rocked him. Gary couldn't believe how much his mum was smiling as she tried to comfort Norton. This wasn't what he wanted at all. "You are a lovely baby, Norton," Bernadette said in her baby sort of voice.

"Now Gary and Robert, are you going to get some tea for Tessie?" Mum asked as she walked into the front room and sat down with Norton.

"OK, Mum," Gary agreed. "I'll make fish fingers and chips."

"Tessie said he's always crying," Robert reminded Bernadette.

"And we know why he's crying now, don't we, Norton?" Bernadette said, chuckling as she spoke.

"Why?" Robert and Gary asked together.

"You've got wind, haven't you, Norton?" Bernadette sat Norton on her lap and gently massaged his back. "This is how we get rid of baby's wind, isn't it, Norton?"

"Teething and wind, that's him," Tessie said.

"Are you two going to get Tessie's tea?" Mum asked, still drawing circles on Norton's back.

"Yes," Gary said reluctantly. Gary and Robert shuffled out to the kitchen.

"It's not working," Robert said. "We'll have to think of..." Just then a muffled explosion interrupted his words, followed by horrified shrieks.

"Tessie! What on earth have you been feeding him?"

Robert and Gary ran into the front room. "Looks like mustard," Robert suggested.

"What's happened?" Gary asked. "It sounded like an explosion."

"What do you *think* has happened?" Bernadette cried. Her smart dress and jacket were covered in the brown and yellow contents of Norton's stomach.

"He sometimes does that," Tessie said, in a chatty tone. "It comes out from both ends at exactly the same time. Mum says it's like squeezing a faulty tube of toothpaste..."

"Tessie!" Mum hissed, interrupting Tessie's comments on the scene. "Don't just stand there. Find me something to wipe up the mess!"

"Oh ... right. Where from?" Tessie asked, confused.

"Go in the kitchen with Gary," Bernadette said, trying hard to stay calm.

"Right, right, Gary ... show me where," Tessie said.

"Is there anything I can do?" Robert asked as Gary and Tessie searched in the kitchen.

Mum sighed, "What a mess, Robert."

"That's babies," Robert agreed. "Nothing but mess. Look at your lovely suit."

"Yes and you can never get these stains off. Even dry cleaning doesn't help..."

"Here we are, we'll soon have this cleared up," Tessie said, briskly, starting to wipe the mess from Bernadette's suit.

"Oh no, Gary!" Bernadette cried. "I don't believe it!"

"What's up now?" Gary asked.

"That's my best linen tablecloth! And those—" she pointed at Tessie wiping the settee clean, "are my best napkins."

"And you can never get them properly clean again – not even with dry cleaning!" Robert added.

"Sorry," Tessie shrank back and dropped the napkins on the carpet. She looked as though she was about to burst into tears.

"Don't cry, Tessie. I'm sorry for being angry. We just need to get this mess cleared up. You hold Norton, I'll go and change," Bernadette said, a little calmer.

Gary and Robert exchanged delighted looks

and put their thumbs up while Tessie worked at wiping the settee.

"It stinks in here," Robert said, waving his arms as if to disperse the smell.

"I'm really sorry – I didn't think Norton would..." Tessie began.

"Don't be sorry. You've done a brilliant job, Tessie," Robert said, smiling.

"Yes, totally brilliant!" Gary agreed. "You *are* wonderful, Tessie!"

A few minutes later, Gary's mum walked back into the room wearing her oldest clothes and carrying a nappy and a clean babygro for Norton. Gary wondered where these baby things had come from, but he said nothing.

Robert, Gary and Tessie watched in stunned silence as a gurgling Norton kicked about on the floor whilst Bernadette changed his nappy and cleaned the mess. "You're brilliant at this, Mrs McNab," Tessie said.

"It's my job, Tessie," Bernadette said.

"My mum's cross with Norton all the time," Tessie confided.

"Babies make you like that," Robert agreed.

"All babies are lovely, Gary," Bernadette said,

fastening Norton's clothes. "Even when they make a terrible mess."

"That's not what my mum says," Tessie said, smiling.

"I'm not surprised, the mess he makes!" Gary mumbled.

"It's probably very hard for her but at least your mum has got you, Tessie. You must be a great help to your mum, looking after Norton and taking him for walks. Isn't Tessie great, boys?"

"Yes," Robert agreed.

Norton began screaming again – real blood-curdling, head-banging screams. "Better go," Tessie said.

"Yes, sounds like he's hungry, Tessie," Bernadette agreed.

"He's always hungry," Tessie said. "Even in the middle of the night..." Tessie's words sank under the weight of Norton's screams.

"What about your tea?" Bernadette asked. "Gary's doing fish fingers and chips."

"I'll come back another day. Thanks, Mrs McNab," Tessie said. "Now I know where you live, I'll call in again." Gary looked at Robert with a horrified expression.

A few minutes later, Robert and Gary sat at the bottom of the stairs. "Did it work?" Robert asked.

"No!" Gary snapped. "It's hard to believe after all the disgusting mess but I think it's made her like babies even more."

"I'm not so sure – she was pleased to hand him back," Robert said, trying to raise Gary's spirits.

"Do you know what I'm really worried about now?" Gary whispered. "Apart from having to clear up—"

"What?" Robert leaned forwards. "Tessie coming for tea another evening?"

"No! I'm worried that if my mum and dad had a baby they'd probably expect me to push it around the streets like Tessie does," Gary said.

"No they wouldn't," Robert said. "Your mum and dad aren't like that."

"Yes they would!"

"Anyways, there won't be a baby because—"

"Do you know, Gary," Bernadette interrupted, "I was so impressed with the way you helped Tessie today. It's made me think – what if you had a little brother or sister? You would be brilliant. I know that already!"

"Told you!" Gary hissed at Robert.

"It won't happen, trust me," Robert said, calmly. "They won't have a baby."

TEN

Gary was very concerned about several things so that evening, he went upstairs, sat down and wrote another list. Father Colum said that writing things down was often the first step to a prayer being answered.

Dear God,
I don't understand a few things:

1 *Why do my mum and dad want another baby when they have got me?*

2 *Why isn't Robert's plan working?*

3 *Where did Mum get that nappy and those clothes from?*

4 *What other baby things has she got in the house already?*

There was one other question in his mind but he didn't want to write it down as it would have made an untidy list. "What if ... there was another baby and I had to look after it, like Tessie?"

A few days after Tessie's visit, Gary was doing his chores. His main job was to tidy up the front room and as he sorted through the papers, he found something else. Something worrying. It was a catalogue. From a baby shop. Gary looked inside the front cover. It made him feel sick.

Welcome to the new Autumn/Winter catalogue
for
Prize-Winning Babies

Yuk! Gary flicked through the catalogue and looked at the disgusting, glossy pictures of hundreds of babies. Some wore just nappies, others clothes. Some sat in bulky prams, others sat in high chairs.

Page after page after page of things needed for babies. It was a bit like Gary's dream – babies crawled all over every page in the catalogue.

Gary just wanted to throw the catalogue into a bin on the way to school so that Mum and Dad would forget all about having a baby. If there were no things to remind them they might think about getting a dog instead.

Gary imagined himself taking a dog for a walk each morning and evening. He imagined a big, yellow dog, a Labrador, holding it back from the main road as they waited to cross over to the park. He even practised how he'd make the dog sit and stay until the traffic lights changed to red.

"Sit!" he shouted and pulled back the lead.

"Gary?" Mum whispered. Gary hadn't noticed her walking into the room. "Have you finished your chores?"

"Yes," Gary sighed, dropping the lead and letting his imaginary dog run off into the park.

"That looked fun," Mum said. "What were you playing?"

"Nothing," Gary said quietly. He was a bit embarrassed that Mum had caught him playing with an imaginary dog.

"Go on, tell me. You used to tell me all about your games. You're not too old for that sort of thing, you know." Sometimes Gary felt that Mum could read his mind.

"To be honest, Mum, I was practising for when we have a dog," he said confidently.

Mum bristled slightly, "We can't get a dog, Gary. We've talked about this before. There's nobody at home all day so it would be cruel to have a dog."

"I could take it for walks in the morning and then after school. We could go to the park," Gary said, persuasively.

"Not at the moment, Gary," Mum said. Gary slumped into the chair, looking irritated and exasperated by his mother's reasoning. "It's not worth falling out about this, Gary. We've never had a dog so it's not as if you're missing anything."

"Suppose so," Gary sighed.

"Let's finish your chores. Come on, I'll help you," Mum said. They started to gather the papers together. Without a word, Gary put the catalogue on top of the papers, ready to place in the recycling bag. "Hang on, hang on," Mum said. "I want to keep this for a few more days."

Why? The question was running around the

inside of Gary's head, but he didn't speak it. He did his chores and then stood for ages watching Mum browse through the catalogue. She seemed to be in a dream world.

"Gary, look at these gorgeous babies. Look at that pram. You wouldn't mind pushing that pram around the park, would you?" Mum said. Gary was visibly stunned as the pages flipped over. "What beautiful high chairs. Now that one would go with the decor in our back room." More pages; flip, flip, flip. "What a gorgeous cot. Look Gary, isn't that wonderful."

Gary didn't speak and his mum didn't seem to notice his horrified silence. The plan wasn't working. The plan was not working. He needed to speak to Robert. Badly.

"The plan isn't working, Robert," Gary announced as they cycled around Robert's street together on Saturday morning.

"What?"

"The plan – the anti-baby plan is just not working," Gary said as he steered his bike on to the footpath, out of the way of a massive lorry.

"How do you mean?" Robert asked.

He told Robert about the baby catalogue. "What do you think?" he asked Robert. "Do you think she's serious or joking?"

"I thought Tessie's baby brother would put your mum off for life. So did my gran," Robert said, thoughtfully.

"It didn't," Gary said.

"My gran will probably know what to do next," Robert said, confidently. "Come on!"

Gran was examining the results of a new recipe when Robert and Gary burst into the kitchen. "We need your help, Gran," he said, almost desperately.

"And I need yours, Robert," she replied, calmly. Gary walked in quietly and sat at the end of the kitchen table. "How are ye, Gary? You're not looking too brilliant. Have you had that bad bug? I believe it's an awful dose. Or is it babies again?"

"Yes," Gary sighed.

"You had the bug?" Gran asked.

"No – well, sort of. After the pies at the football I had gut rot. But it's babies again. I can't believe it. I thought Tessie's baby brother would put her off."

"Well, I have just the thing that will cheer you up, no mistake, Gary," Gran said, sympathetically.

"What's that?" Gary asked.

"Granite cake!"

"Granite cake?" Robert said, amazed at the idea. "It won't break my teeth will it?"

"I hope not, otherwise we'll have to sue *Woman's Life* Magazine, for it's there I saw the recipe." Gran started to cut the cake, placed proudly in the middle of the table.

Gary thought that it looked like granite – it was sort of grey with darker flecks. "What are these bits?" he asked, pointing at the darker flecks.

"Would you believe it, Gary, they're chocolate chips!" Gran said.

Gary bit into the cake cautiously at first, but then, "Mmm, this is really, really delicious," he announced.

"The best yet," Robert agreed.

"Good. I'm glad. Now maybe that'll take your mind off wretched babies for a few minutes!"

Robert and Gary laughed even though their mouths were full of granite. As they chewed, Gran talked. "When I was up in the Post Office yesterday, I was talking to Mrs Kavanagh who lives down near Roman Avenue. You know her, don't you, Robert?"

"No," Robert said.

"You do, you do!" Gran insisted. "Anyway, the daughter was going on and on to her mum about having another baby..."

"She must be mad," Gary said.

"Well now, whether she was mad or not, the mum got really, really fed up so one day she took the daughter into town, into that big new shop in the Cornmarket..."

"I know the one, it's massive..." Robert said.

"That's it, that's the one," Gran continued, "and she took out a calculator and she said, 'now let's see how much it would cost to buy a pram and a pushchair and all the rest of the blessed paraphernalia'. So they walked around with the old calculator and at the end of it, she said to her daughter, 'That's how much it would cost for a new baby'."

"And what did the daughter say?" Gary asked.

"She was amazed. But, anyways, the mother said to her: 'For that amount of money the whole family can go to Majorca for a fortnight. So what is it to be – a new baby or a fortnight in Majorca?'"

"I know what I'd say," Robert interrupted.

"Indeed you do, you're not daft, Robert. So the mum went down to the holiday shop that minute and booked a holiday," Gran finished.

Robert and Gary continued to eat their granite cake in silence. After a few minutes, Gary said, "Mum wouldn't come into town with me like that."

"I know what we can do!" Robert announced, confidently. "We could show your mum and dad how much all these things would cost!"

"Good for you," Gran said, clapping her hands. "That's the idea. You have to be practical!"

"How can we do it?" Gary asked, unsure about Robert's enthusiasm. "How can we make it work this time?"

ELEVEN

Robert and Gary caught the bus into town and spent ages checking new computer games and videos, putting off the moment when they would have to go into the dreaded shop. Then they had a burger and chips.

Eventually, they stood outside the new de luxe Parentcare shop, sheepishly checking to see if anyone they knew was around. They didn't want to be seen actually walking into this place.

Moments after they did go into the shop, they were stopped by a burly security guard. "What are you two up to?" he asked in a hostile voice. "Applying for the job as bouncer?"

Gary laughed. Robert said, "No," in a flat voice.

"Well, I think you're in the wrong shop. What would you want with baby clothes?" The security guard pointed towards the door.

"We're doing a project," Robert said, quickly taking a pencil from his rucksack.

"What for?"

"It's for school. To see how much a baby costs," Gary replied, smartly.

"Bit young for that, aren't you?"

"No, I don't think so..." Robert said. He was slightly irritated with this.

"Get a catalogue," the security guard said. "And do your sums at home!"

"Could you tell us where they are, please?" Gary asked, very politely.

"That great unmissable pile in the middle of the shop!" the security guard snapped.

"Thank you," Gary said. "It's very kind of you to be so helpful."

"Two pounds each!" the security guard shouted over. People were beginning to look at Gary and Robert.

"Two pounds!" Gary hissed. "That's robbery. We're not even buying anything."

"Yeah, but if we need it, you've got to buy it,"

Robert whispered.

"I haven't got two pounds," Gary said.

"How much have you got?" Robert asked.

"About a pound but..."

"I've got a pound, too. You can pay me back again and we'll have to walk home," Robert planned.

"I can't! My mum will go mad!"

"Are you buying that or not!" the security guard questioned.

"Yes," Robert said.

"No!" Gary shouted.

"Don't be such a wimp, Gary. Your mum won't even know if you've walked home or caught the bus so ... do you want this plan to work or not?" Robert argued.

"I suppose so," Gary agreed.

"Well, give us your pound then!"

"I still say it's robbery," Gary mumbled.

"It's a sound investment if it stops the babies in your house!"

"I hope it works after all this money," Gary said.

"It will, trust me," Robert said, reassuringly. "Now let's get out of here before we're spotted!"

Gran was astounded when she heard that they had paid good money for *a catalogue*. "Well I'm telling you this, I wouldn't have paid!"

"We had to," Robert said.

"I would have told them that I'd pay money when I bought something. It's ridiculous!"

"I told you we shouldn't have paid," Gary said.

"And get done for stealing?" Robert replied.

"When I had your mother, there was no such thing as a catalogue for baby stuff. It's a big old commercial con-trick!" Gran decreed. "When I see those girls walking around town, only children themselves, pushing prams that cost a fortune in lime green and pink and purple..."

"If Mum and Dad knew how expensive prams are – do you think they'd be put off having a baby?" Gary asked, interrupting Gran.

"They might ... they might indeed. But there's no need for all this expense, Gary," Gran said. "At one time, everyone would knit for the child and make a layette for the first few months..." Gran explained.

"What's a layette?" Robert asked.

"I'll show you," Gran said, flicking through the catalogue. "Here it is," she pointed to a page of tiny babies draped in white baggy clothes and knitted hats and boots. "Only it's not called a layette any more. Well it wouldn't be – it's called a Starter Pack now. They make a baby sound like a blessed construction kit!" Gran was shaking her head now. "And look at the price of it. Fifty pounds for a few bits of white clothing..."

"That would put them off," Robert said.

"But your mum could make all these, Gary," Gran said.

"No, no. I don't want her to make anything because I don't want her to have a baby, remember?" Gary insisted.

"I don't suppose she would have the time to make anything, she's that busy with her work and..." Gran paused. "Arrah, Gary, she won't have a baby. She's far too busy. Your mum seems to love her job too much."

"But if we were to make sure – wouldn't it be good to let her know how expensive it is to have a baby?" Robert asked.

"It doesn't have to be – she could buy a second-hand pram out of the paper and she could, as I said, make all the lovely little clothes. That wouldn't be too dear," Gran said gently, warming to the idea. "Indeed I could help her out by making a few things for her, that would save a few bob..."

"No Gran!" Robert interrupted. "You're supposed to be helping *us*, not them!"

"Oh I'm sorry, Gary. I was getting a bit carried away."

"That's OK," Gary said.

"Now what is it, exactly, that you want me to do?" Gran asked.

"We want to know which things in this book my mum and dad will need to buy for a baby."

"Right!" Gran said, decisively. "Pass the book here and I'll start!"

Robert and Gary worked for ages on Sunday afternoon, typing the price list they'd compiled with Gran's help, into the computer.

At the top of the list, Gary wrote a short message for his parents:

Babies are very, very expensive and they soon grow out of all these things. Look at this list:

The Cost of Babies

Starter pack	50.00
Sheets	17.99
Blankets	16.98
Cot bumper	22.99
Wallpaper for nursery	55.00
Changing mat	7.00
De luxe bouncing cradle	27.99
Electric swing	94.99
De luxe gliding crib	99.99
Cot	199.00
Mattress	54.99
Sound and vision monitor	299.00
Bath set	30.00
Baby box	18.00
Pram	429.00
Changing bag	30.00
Car seat	69.99
Baby carrier	44.99
High chair	44.99
Total	£ 1612.89

This works out at just over one season ticket for City
or
A new football strip for every week of the season
or
A fortnight in Majorca for all of us!

How will we even be able to buy food if we have to pay for all of this?

Babies are far too expensive for this family. If we have one it might mean starvation for the rest of us.

You have been warned!

TWELVE

On Tuesday morning Mr Doyle's classroom had been transformed. Coloured tissue paper covered the windows giving a pastel glow to the room and desks had been moved to the edge of the class. The chairs were placed in a large circle.

Gary liked the music that played gently on Mr Doyle's stereo. It raised his spirits a little. The music also had a strange effect on the whole class. At first, when they arrived in their changed room, they were chatting and excited, but as the music hypnotised the children, the noise subsided. The few conversations that did continue were calmed by Father Colum's outstretched hand and his gentle, "Shush, shush."

Most of the children took a deep, relaxing breath and settled into their places as Father Colum began to speak. "Remember the other day, I asked you to write down on a piece of paper something that you really wanted to pray for. Remember that?" The class murmured a positive response and nodded as Father Colum looked at their prayers. "Would anyone like to share their prayer request?"

Tessie started to speak, slowly at first. "I told God about how I always have to look after our little baby and my mum never seems to have much time for me any more because she's got this illness that people sometimes get after having babies..."

"What's that?" Robert asked.

"It's like they get very sad and they don't want to do anything and they're not interested in anything," Tessie replied.

"Oh no," Gary mumbled.

"I kept wishing that the baby hadn't been born because then my mum would be all right but now I'm trying to help my mum a bit more and she looks like she's getting a bit better. And some people in my class have been kindly helping me..."

Gary and Robert squirmed in their chairs.

"You know, children, you mentioned your

families a lot in your prayers – especially brothers and sisters. From what you're saying, they can be a great joy to you but they can also be a huge pain..."

"You're not kidding," Kieran interrupted.

"This morning, in our little service, we'll all light a candle and think about the prayer requests we have made. Perhaps we could all think about our families – how we could make them better."

Father Colum passed the candles around. "You'll see that each candle has a paper collar – that's to make sure that the wax doesn't drip on to your clothes. But we have to be careful and hold the candles straight, just in case."

The children giggled nervously. This was a new and unusual thing to do. Father Colum then placed a bowl of water in the middle of the room. "We're going to use this water later on – it's a sort of symbol..."

Father Colum lit the first candle and asked the children to light one another's candles. "Hold your candles carefully," Father Colum advised. "Watch as they burn and, one by one, I'd like you to say what you have been praying for."

Gary began to sweat. "What shall I say?" he

thought. He closed his eyes for a moment. He wanted to concentrate. He had to be honest or his prayer might not be answered.

"Let's start with Stephen," Father Colum suggested.

"I've written a prayer about my little brother," Stephen began.

"What shall I say?" Gary thought. He wasn't listening to Stephen. He wasn't looking at anyone or anything. He didn't notice the paper collar on his candle lean against Robert's candle. He didn't see it catch fire. Robert jumped up.

"Gary! You eejit!" Robert shouted.

"Help! Fire!" Tessie cried.

"It's all right," Father Colum said, trying to calm Tessie.

"No it's not! Gary's on fire!" Tessie cried again.

Robert and Gary tried hard to blow out the flames on the paper collar. "He'll be all right in a minute," Robert said, unconvincingly.

Tessie wouldn't wait. "Stand back!" she yelled, picking up the bowl of water.

"No Tessie!" Robert and Gary howled together.

Too late. Tessie hurled the water at Robert and Gary. The other children watched in stunned silence as Gary and Robert screamed.

"Tessie!"

Father Colum gestured for the other children to sit down. "Blow out your candles, too. We'll have to leave this for today."

Gary and Robert wiped the water from their faces and shook their heads. "You're an idiot, Tessie," Robert hissed.

"You two look a right pair," Tessie said, ignoring Robert and smiling at the spectacle of the two drenched boys. "Aren't you glad I saved your life?"

"Tessie, you were very good," Father Colum agreed.

"One good turn deserves another," she said.

"It would have to happen to you pair, wouldn't it?" Father Colum said, shaking his head and smiling. The other children laughed as Gary and Robert tried to dry themselves off.

Mr Doyle came back into the classroom. "I heard all the commotion and wondered what was going on," he explained. "We'd better get you two changed. Let's go down to the medical room."

"Need any help?" Tessie offered.

"No!" Robert and Gary shouted together. "Leave us alone!"

"Imagine," Gary thought, under his wet hair and soaking jumper. "Imagine if I had a baby sister and she turned out like Tessie." He shivered even more.

THIRTEEN

> Dear Parents,
>
> Come and join the Celebration
> on Thursday evening
> at seven o'clock.
>
> Share in the joy and the prayers
> of your children.

"That's a lovely idea," Bernadette McNab said as she read Father Colum's invitation. "We've heard so much about him. Although I hope he isn't going to use candles!"

"He's certainly inspired you, Gary. I've never known you be so enthusiastic about school," Dad said as he stood beside Gary who was trying to do his homework. "What are you doing, son?"

"Maths," Gary said, gloomily.

"Your mum says," Dad said, his voice full of meaning, "that your Maths is really, really improving and you're using it in real life situations!"

Gary turned and looked at his dad with a quizzical expression. "What do you mean?"

"The exorbitant cost of babies?" Dad said.

"Oh very funny, not!" Gary said, almost sneering.

When Mum was out of the room Dad moved towards Gary and said, "You certainly made me think, Gary. I wouldn't want to go without a season ticket for City."

"Really," Gary said, his eyes sparkling with hope.

"Yes," said Dad. "But don't let on to your mum."

"What?" Mum said as she walked back into the room.

"I was saying that was a brilliant away win for City on Saturday. It's like Gary's prayers certainly are being answered," Dad said, sheepishly.

"I told you, Dad. You made fun of me but Father

Colum said if you really pray hard for something, your prayers will be answered," Gary said.

"So what are you praying for now that prayer has been answered?" Gary's mum asked as she folded and sorted some clothes.

Gary hesitated for a moment. "I wish Father Colum could stay for ever," he said, trying to change the subject of what he was praying for.

"It wouldn't be the same," Mum said. "You'd soon get used to him and he wouldn't be special any more."

"I suppose," Gary agreed. "But I wish he could stay a bit longer."

"You can write to him," Dad suggested, "when he returns to his home."

"Good idea," Mum said.

"Let him know how City are getting on, send him match reports, that sort of thing."

"Yes. It still won't be the same," Gary murmured before settling back to his Maths homework.

Gary found it hard to concentrate. Inside he was tingling with excitement. His dad had gone off the idea of having a baby! He knew it would work if he mentioned the cost of season tickets. Dad was clearly having second thoughts. Fantastic! Now it was up to Gary and Robert to change Mum's mind. Dad was on their side ... almost.

"Storm heaven!" That's what Father Colum had said. "If you want God to help you in some way, then you need to storm heaven. Keep reminding God about your prayer. Say it over and over again. Nag God – in the nicest possible way."

Gary closed his eyes tightly. "We've been helping you along with this, God," he silently prayed. "And it's beginning to work. Dad has changed sides – a bit of our prayer has been answered. Thanks. Now can you do something about my mum?"

Gary couldn't wait to tell Robert and his gran about Dad's change of heart. Now they had to think of something for Mum. Quickly.

It was, everyone agreed, a brilliant evening. The music, the singing, the quiet times and the fun. "You'll remember this for a long, long time," Bernadette said.

After the service there was lots of food and Father Colum shook hands with every mum and dad and told them how proud they must be to have such a lovely child.

Eventually, Father Colum reached Gary's

parents. "Congratulations on your wedding!" he said.

"Thanks," Bernadette and Eugene replied, smiling.

"And on your lovely son. You must be so proud of him," Father Colum continued.

"We are," they replied.

"Thanks for all you've done in school. You've really inspired Gary. He's been praying all the time," Bernadette said.

"And City are winning!" Father Colum said as he moved away to the next group of parents.

"Isn't he gorgeous?" Robert's gran said to Gary's mum and dad.

"Yes," Bernadette said, dreamily. "And he's such a lovely, kind personality."

"It's no wonder the kids are praying and singing and dancing. Sure, he'd make a stone laugh," Gran said, smiling.

Gary was standing some distance away eating cakes and laughing with Robert, Kieran and Stephen. He suddenly noticed Robert's gran and his mum talking to one another. "Hey Robert, look! Your gran won't say anything to my mum, will she?"

"Course not," Robert said.

"Shall we stand near them, just in case?"

"Stand near who?" Father Colum asked, appearing from nowhere. "Is it some girls you want to stand near?"

"No!" Robert and Gary said, as if they were about to be sick.

"We want to check what my gran is saying to Gary's mum and dad," Robert said.

"Whatever for?" Father Colum said in a mischievous voice. "What have you two been up to? You're a right pair of holy terrors, aren't you?"

Gary and Robert quickly told Father Colum about their plans to stop any baby in Gary's house. He listened intently as Gary told him how he dreaded the thought of a new baby. They were interrupted by a clanging bell. It was their headmaster.

"Boys and girls, mums and dads, grannies and grandads, aunts and uncles and friends. I want to say a few words to Father Colum..."

As the headmaster spoke, Robert's gran looked over at Gary and winked as if to say, "Don't worry. I've kept your secret safe."

"Thanks!" the headmaster said, firmly. "Thank you for all you have done for our school. We've had a wonderful fortnight, haven't we?"

There was a cacophony of shouting, cheering and clapping as Father Colum went on to the stage for his presentation.

Gary felt so sad that Father Colum was going. He had really listened to the children when they had talked about their lives and he made school bearable with his music and stories. It was a totally different place with Father Colum. He would miss him.

"Goodbye," Gary said, eventually shaking hands with Father Colum. "I'll write to you."

"I'll look forward to your letters," Father Colum said, ruffling Gary's hair. "And yours too, Robert."

"We'll write, don't worry," Gary said.

"And let me know how things are going ... you terrors..." Father Colum said, smiling broadly, "...on the baby front!"

FOURTEEN

The next week at school was dull and boring without Father Colum. Gary couldn't wait for the weekend. "Can I go round to Robert's on Saturday morning?" Gary asked as soon as he arrived home on Friday.

"No, I want us to do something together, as a family," Gary's mum said. "I want us all to go shopping."

"*Shopping?*" Gary asked in amazement.

"Yes. Like you did last Saturday, with Robert. Remember?" Mum said.

"That was different," Gary said. "Mum, I hate shopping and I'll be moaning all afternoon. Please can I go and play with Robert?"

"What do you think, Eugene?" Mum asked.

"Gary's got a point. It's bad enough shopping without him trailing around after us, moaning all the time. Yes, you can play with Robert."

"Thanks, Dad!"

Robert had just finished mending a puncture when Gary arrived. "D'you fancy going up the BMX track?" Robert asked.

"OK – if there's nothing else to do..." Gary replied, hesitantly.

"Gran said it's *well* slippy and they've put some new bits in..."

"What's your gran been doing up at the BMX track?" Gary asked, interrupting Robert.

"She was walking the dog."

"You haven't got a dog," Gary said, "have you?"

"It's next door's dog. Gran's looking after it while they're away on holiday."

"Lucky thing," Gary sighed. "I wish we had a dog."

"So you've said about a million times! Shall we go on the BMX track or what?" Robert asked again.

"All right – but I'm not to get dirty," Gary said.

Robert smiled.

Everyone had heard about the new ramps at the BMX track so Gary and Robert had to wait for ages to take their turn. Robert went first, attacking the uphill parts and carefully coming downhill. He didn't want to come off his bike, there were too many people watching.

Gary followed, again with a good deal of caution. In between their turns, Gary and Robert leaned over their handlebars and talked about bikes, school and their 'no-baby' plan.

"Gran says that you need to remind your mum that babies are really hard work and she says that you never get a decent night's sleep and your clothes are always covered in baby milk," Robert advised.

"Why don't babies sleep at night?" Gary asked, keeping an eye on the line of bikes in front of them.

"I don't know," Robert said, as he was trying to do a standing wheelie. "They just always wake up screaming, wanting something to eat and then their mucky nappies changed."

"Yuk!"

Then it was Gary's turn again. He felt angry at the thought of a baby waking him at night just to have its nappy changed. He forgot about the slippy bit over near the gully. He lost control of his bike and spun off into the bushes.

"Yo!" the crowd of boys shouted. "More, more!" When Gary emerged from the bushes, his face was scratched and twigs and bits of leaf were caught up in his hair. He wiped the leaves away from his face and, in the process, left two great streaks of mud across his cheek and nose.

"You look a right sight," Robert said, before taking his go.

Gary was cross with himself for thinking about babies when he should have been concentrating on the track. But it was a bad bit and Robert made exactly the same mistake only he went over the handlebars and straight into an enormous muddy puddle in the gully. The waiting onlookers cheered.

"You look a right sight," Gary said, imitating Robert.

"I'm freezing! I'm going home!" Robert announced.

"Don't be so wet!" Gary argued, then laughed at his remark.

"Very funny!" Robert said, unable to smile.

"Let's stay for a bit longer," Gary suggested. "You'll soon dry off, Robert."

"No, I'm cold and..."

"OK," Gary agreed. "Let's go home."

Robert's gran was amazed to see the two boys back so soon – and so dirty.

"Robert, you have never changed, not since you were a toddler," she said, shaking her head. "Come in and get dried quickly and we'll see what we have in the cake tin."

"I'm freezing, Gran," Robert said, his words muffled by the towel he was using to dry his hair and face.

"This takes me back, Robert. You were a little monkey when you were a little boy – always into mischief and *always* dirty!"

Robert groaned. "I was a lovely baby though, wasn't I?"

"You were not!" Gran replied. "You didn't sleep for weeks. That's probably why you have no brothers or sisters. Honest to God, if only people had better memories about how awful babies are at night, there wouldn't be half the babies born!" Gran said.

Gary smiled at Gran's words. Robert's face screwed up into a quizzical expression like he was trying to think something through.

"What did you say, Gran?" he asked.

"I said, if people had better memories about how awful babies are at night, there wouldn't be half the babies born," Gran repeated.

There was a long pause and then Robert spoke, very slowly. "That's given me an idea, Gary. A really brilliant idea. About a new plan!"

"Tell us," Gary said.

Robert began to explain. "You just have to remind them about what it's like to be woken at night..."

"How can we do that?" Gary questioned.

"Well..." Robert began, "listen to this..."

FIFTEEN

Gary was too tired on Saturday night to carry out the first part of Robert's plan. He felt in a bad mood all evening. City had scored five goals – their best win of the season – and he had missed it. All because Mum wanted Dad to go shopping with her.

"There will be other good wins," Dad consoled him.

"Not as good as this," Gary said.

"I promise I won't let that happen again," Dad said in a hushed voice.

"We've still missed their best win of the season," Gary said, unwilling to be comforted. "What did you buy, anyway?"

"Nothing much," Mum replied quickly.

Nothing much? Gary couldn't believe that they'd missed City's best win for ages for 'nothing much'.

He was pleased that he had a 'plan' for the next few days. In a way, he wanted to pay Mum and Dad back for making him miss the match.

On Monday night he went to bed early and set his alarm for half-past one. Gary didn't hear it but his Mum did and she turned it off, muttering loudly about Gary's inaccurate setting of the clock. Gary fell straight back to sleep and didn't wake until the following morning.

Gary heard the alarm at midnight on Tuesday. He switched it off and started groaning, quietly at first and then really noisily. "Mum!" he howled. She was fast asleep. "Mum!" again only much louder.

"What? What is it? My God, I was in the middle of a dream," Mum shouted as she ran into Gary's room. "What is it, love?"

Gary writhed about, dramatic and totally convincing. "It's my stomach," he muttered, clutching the middle of his pyjamas.

"Oh no, you look dreadful," Mum said.

Dad appeared. "It's not appendicitis, is it?"

"I hope not," Mum said, "although he does appear to be in terrible pain."

"Shall we take him down to casualty, just to be on the safe side?"

Gary was alarmed. He started to scale down the writhing about. "It's easing off a bit."

"That sounds like appendicitis to me," Dad said. "It gets really bad and then it eases off a bit. That's appendicitis..."

"No, it's OK, it's getting better," Gary said.

"I know. I'll get a hot water bottle and you put it against the pain and if it doesn't get any better after an hour, we *will* go to casualty."

"Good idea, Mum," Gary said, almost forgetting his suffering pose. Dad looked a little puzzled. "I'll probably be feeling better soon."

With the warm bottle close to his non-aching stomach, Gary fell asleep very quickly. Eugene and Bernadette, however, were awake for hours, in case the appendicitis pain returned. "We'd better stay awake, we might have to go to casualty."

On Wednesday night, Gary decided to suffer from something that would not involve a trip to the local hospital. So, at two-thirty he woke with toothache.

"Aah!" he screamed. "Mum and Dad my tooth's killing me."

Dad was first on the scene. "Gary – if this is your idea of a joke at two-thirty in the morning..."

"My tooth hurts!" Gary shouted.

"Two-thirty, tooth hurty! Very funny, Gary!"

"No it does, it hurts like mad," Gary said, struggling to look in pain.

"Cloves," Mum said. "That's the remedy for toothache. I'll go and get you one, Gary." Gary had to keep up the pretence of an aching face whilst Dad watched over him and Mum ran down the stairs to the kitchen.

"Strange this ... stomachache last night, toothache tonight. I wonder what is going on in your head, son," Dad said. Gary's face looked strained with his toothache.

The clove tasted disgusting but Gary had to place it against his non-hurting tooth until Mum and Dad were safely out of the room. Then he spat it as high as he could. It landed on the cold hot water bottle.

On Thursday night, Gary shouted out from a nightmare at three o'clock. "Help!"

Mum ran into his room again. "What is it?" she said, breathless and irritated.

"A bad dream," Gary said, clinging on to his mum's arm.

"What was the dream," Mum said, trying to be sympathetic.

"I can't remember..."

"Try!" Mum snapped.

"I think ... I think it was ... yes, you had given me away to another family. One with lots of children. It was awful. They were making me do all the work ... It was such a bad dream. Sorry for waking you, Mum."

"It was a dream, Gary, that's all. Now try to go back to sleep," Mum said, tucking the covers around Gary. "By the morning you will have forgotten all about it."

"It won't come true, will it?" Gary asked.

"No," said Mum firmly.

On Friday morning, Gary heard the confirmation that his plan had worked. They thought Gary was upstairs getting ready, out of earshot. "I'm totally exhausted," Dad said. "All this waking in the middle of the night."

"Yes," Mum agreed. "I don't know what's up with Gary, he has suffered a lot this week."

"Brings back awful memories of when he was a baby – always waking at night. Terrible memories..."

"It's enough to put someone off babies for life,"

Mum said. "Do you remember when we used to say that? It's probably why Gary is an only child. He was so difficult at night."

"Yes, how could I forget? All those nights watching dreadful films and awful cookery programmes trying to get him to sleep," Dad agreed.

"Yess!" Gary punched the air. "I've done it! I've done it!" He couldn't wait to tell Robert.

"Robert!" Gary howled at the top of his voice, trying to make his friend turn around. "We've done it!"

"What?" Robert asked when Gary caught up with him.

"We've done it! Your plan has worked!"

"Waking them up in the night?" Robert said, brighter than before.

"Yes!"

"Brilliant! I knew it would work," Robert said.

"Mum said it's enough to put anyone off babies for life!"

"Excellent!"

"I'm going to write to Father Colum this weekend and tell him," Gary said, brightly.

"Good idea," Robert said, encouraging his friend.

"No more babies any more," Gary sang to the tune of one of his mum's old favourites. Robert joined in and the pair ran to school singing, "No more babies any more!"

32, Ramsey Grove,
Leicester.
Saturday.

Dear Father Colum,

It is about two weeks since you left and me and Robert have missed you. We really liked the talks you did every day, and then that service when we sat around holding the candles and we talked about our families – even though me and Robert got soaking wet!

One of the things I wanted to tell you is that City have done brilliantly since me and Robert started praying for them. First of all they won against United and Tyrone played another blinder. He was here, he was there, he was everywhere. And he scored two fantastic goals. The first one he was playing in defence and he got the ball. He made an amazing run down the centre and then he beat two United players before he was tripped in the penalty box. It was a penalty, a definite penalty but the ref said no – so we all started shouting, 'Where's your specs, ref?' One bloke shouted, 'You need a white stick you useless...' I can't repeat it 'cause it's swearing. Tyrone was pleading with the ref for a bit while Rosie went to take the corner (you know, Theodore Rose, the one who plays on the inside left for City), so then Tyrone moved into a space – the United players were a bit stunned that they hadn't given away a penalty. The corner sailed over the mouth of the goal and Tyrone blasted it in. One–nil! In the second half, Tyrone was tripped again by the same United player in the penalty box and this time he was given a penalty which he scored! Then all the City fans were saying that the ref wasn't too bad. In midweek City played away in a cup match, first leg. They drew but we'll probably hammer them on the home leg. Do you get upset when you hear people swearing at football matches? It must be hard for you. On Saturday, City were at home again but my mum and dad wanted to go shopping so we didn't go to the match. I was seriously fed up because City won five-nil and Tyrone scored a hat-trick of three goals. I was really fed up with Mum and Dad for spoiling my chance to see City's best win for years.

That's all for now.

Yours sincerely,

Gary McNab.

PS I think my mum and dad have almost gone off the idea of having another baby. Remember how you told us to help God to answer prayers? Well, me and Robert did that. Robert is brilliant at plans.

PPS Tessie's mum has had to go into hospital so Tessie has extra baby duty to do. All the rest of the class are fine and they are going to write you long letters like this.

SIXTEEN

The first week of November, Gary began to notice something really strange. Things had settled down at home. Mum had stopped trying too hard to make them seem like a proper family and Dad was much more relaxed about being back.

On Guy Fawkes night it was the same as every year – Dad took Gary to the school bonfire. "Do you want to come this year, Bernadette?" Dad asked.

"No! You know I hate fireworks," Mum replied, smiling.

"Well you rest yourself," Dad advised as they left the house.

"Is Mum all right?" Gary asked, on the way to the bonfire.

"Yes," Dad said, curiously. "Why shouldn't she be?"

"You told her to rest. Is she OK?"

"Yes – she's just having a difficult time at work. Lots of babies but not enough midwives. Anyway," dad said, rubbing his hands together with enthusiasm, "Let's just enjoy the bonfire!"

"I'm glad you're back, Dad," Gary said, speaking his thoughts.

Dad was a little taken aback. "So am I," Dad said. "I'm pleased we're a family again."

"But not the sort of family who have to go shopping together," Gary said.

"And miss City's best win in years!"

"Yes!" Gary agreed.

"We're a good family, Gary. We don't live in one another's pockets or suffocate one another, do we?"

"No ... and we're just the right size, eh Dad?"

Dad didn't answer for a moment.

"Eh Dad?" Gary said again.

Dad smiled.

This was the best bonfire ever. The best fireworks, the biggest fire, the tastiest sausages and the funniest guy. Gary would always remember it because that was the evening when he felt that everything was just right in the world. Just perfect. Mum and Dad back together, Dad standing next to him in front of a magnificent bonfire and Mum back home, resting after a hard day, delivering other people's babies.

Yes, things were better than Gary could ever remember on that Guy Fawkes night.

When they returned home, Mum was in bed and she didn't answer when Eugene and Gary shouted up the stairs. The following evening she went to bed straight after tea and that was the pattern for several days.

Gary began to feel worried, and he was even more concerned because it seemed as though Dad *wasn't* worried. In the mornings, Mum didn't come down to breakfast. Dad took her a drink and a biscuit and then she came down all dressed for work.

Gary began to imagine that Mum had a terminal disease. "Just my luck," he confided to Robert one day. "For Mum and Dad to get back together and then for Mum to die."

He told Robert's gran about Mum's symptoms.

She shook her head slowly. "Do you think she's dying?" Gary asked her.

"I think it's worse than that," Gran said.

"How could anything be worse than Mum dying?" Gary asked.

"Maybe you should ask her yourself," Gran advised.

As the days went by and the leaves gathered into huge piles in the garden, Gary kept trying to ask his mum if she was dying. He couldn't ask her, he didn't want to know the truth.

He asked Dad. "What is up with Mum? Why won't she have meals with us or stay up late any more?"

Dad hesitated before he answered and then when he started to speak, he stopped again, looked down at his palms, as if searching for the right words and then said, "It's a bit hard to say at the moment."

"Will she be all right, Dad?" Gary asked, desperate for more information.

"Probably," Dad replied.

Gary watched his Dad collapse into the sofa and switch on the television. He didn't seem to be all that concerned. How could he flop so easily into the sofa when Mum was seriously ill? How could he watch a stupid programme about vets rescuing swans when Mum was failing by the minute? Why did things go wrong so quickly? Why weren't they allowed a little more happiness together as a family?

Gary went to his room early. He knelt beside the bed and prayed, "Please God, make my mum better. If there is a God, make her well again so that we can all be together as a family."

He slept better that night. Safe in the knowledge that most of his prayers were answered. Like a miracle, his mum came down to breakfast the following morning.

"Mum?"

"I'm so much better today," she said brightly.

"Are you all right now?" Gary asked cautiously.

"I'm getting there, Gary."

Mum stopped preparing her breakfast and sat at the table next to him. "This evening we'll have a proper chat about why I've been so ill and then you'll begin to understand."

"Tell me now," Gary pleaded.

"No. I want to be around so I can answer all your questions, and that won't happen if you have to go straight off to school."

"But I'll be worried all day," Gary pleaded.

"No you won't. I promise, I'm not going to die and I am getting better. Promise."

Gary was not convinced. He walked slowly to school, dreading the news that the evening might bring.

"I wish Father Colum was still here," Gary confided to Robert during breaktime at school.

"Yes, so do I," Robert agreed.

"He understood us," Gary said.

"We didn't have to do Maths and English when he was here," Robert said.

"He listened to us, he taught us how to pray."

"What's up with you?" Robert asked. "You've gone *dead* holy."

"Well, I might need to get holy if my mum dies!"

"She won't die," Robert said, trying to comfort his friend.

"They're going to tell me this evening," Gary said.

"Tell you what?"

"What's up with her. It's probably an awful, awful disease," Gary said.

"Well at least you'll be able to have time off school," said Robert.

"Robert!" Gary said, irritated with his friend's

consoling words. "This is dead serious."

"Sorry," Robert said, gently. "I was only trying to help."

"I think only God can help us now," Gary said, in a forlorn voice.

"Right, Gary," said Robert. "If he can work miracles for City, it won't take too much to do something for your mum!"

Gary smiled and patted his friend on the shoulder. "Thanks, mate."

SEVENTEEN

That evening, Bernadette and Eugene sat either side of Gary on the settee, looking at one another and then back at him. He waited to hear the news of his mum's impending death or a slow, lingering illness that would make his life miserable for many years to come.

"Gary, brace yourself for this news," Dad said.

Mum put her hand on his arm. "Gary, our family is going to be bigger, much bigger."

Bigger? What did she mean? Bosnian orphans? Grandparents coming to live with them? "What do you mean?" Gary asked.

"We're going to have an extension to our family," Mum explained.

"A conservatory?" Gary asked, hopefully.

"No," Mum said, smiling. "Twins!"

"*What?*" Gary was confused. What did she mean, 'twins'?

"Me, you and Dad – we're going to have twins," Mum said.

"Where from?" Gary asked, still not understanding.

"I'm expecting twins, Gary," Mum said, getting a little impatient.

"Twins?" Gary said, disbelieving. "*Twins?*"

"Yes ... twins," Mum said, slowly and deliberately.

"How did this happen?" Gary asked.

"Well ... it's a long story, love. Maybe you and I can have a little chat about it later," Dad said. "Although I must admit, I thought you would have known about all this by now."

"No, I don't mean *that*," Gary protested. "I mean, how can you be expecting twins when you've been so ill?"

"The twins made me ill," Mum said.

"That's terrible," Gary replied.

"It's perfectly normal, Gary. A good sign and I'm getting over it now," Mum said, brightly.

"Tell us, Gary. Tell us honestly – how do you

feel about the news?" Dad asked.

They waited an age for Gary's response. For a few minutes he was speechless.

"Go on, Gary," Mum prompted him. "What do you think? How do you feel?"

"I'm gutted," Gary said. "Absolutely gutted!"

"What do you mean, Gary?" Mum said, the smile vanishing from her face.

"I'm gutted, Mum. You heard me! That's exactly what I mean," Gary replied.

"Look, Gary – can you try and be happy with us?" said Dad.

"Can I go to bed now?" Gary asked, ignoring his dad's question.

"Gary, wait—" Mum said. "I thought we could have a little celebration together."

"I just want to go to bed," Gary said again.

"All right, Gary, you go to bed," Mum said. "I'll be up in a few minutes to tuck you in."

Gary walked slowly up the stairs and into his room. He looked at the football posters and shelves of match programmes and magazines as if he was bidding them goodbye. Then he threw himself on to his bed, face down. He wrapped his hands around his head and rocked himself for a few moments.

"I'm finished with you, God," he whispered. Then, "I won't cry, I'm not going to cry." But the tears came. First slowly, cooling Gary's angry, red face. Then stomach sobs escaped and eventually, Gary howled. He turned over on to his back, kicked the wall and pulled at his curtain until it came away from the rail.

Gary jumped up from the bed and snatched at the City posters, tearing them in half. He thumped the wall and smacked the top of his computer.

Mum walked into the room. She took Gary's hand and made him sit on his bed. "Come on, Gary, calm down. It's best if we talk about this." Dad appeared at the doorway.

"You NEVER listen to me!" Gary shouted.

"We do," Mum said, unconvincingly.

"No you don't. I HATE babies. I said I didn't want one and now you're going to have *two*..."

"It's a bit of a shock, but you'll get used to the idea," Dad suggested.

"No I won't! I hate babies. You never, ever listen to me! I wanted a dog but you said they were too much trouble. You wanted a baby and I tried to show you ... that they were worse than having a dog."

"Show us?" Dad said, puzzled.

"I'll be like Tessie. I won't be able to do my school work. I won't be able to watch City ... Dad, you agreed with me. Now you're a traitor!"

"Is that why you asked Tessie to tea?" Mum said.

"Yes! Now we're going to have two screaming brats like Norton who'll keep us awake all night and take over our house."

"And then they will grow into nice brothers and sisters and you'll be glad that we made the decision to have another..." Dad said, trying to be reasonable.

"Sisters! What an embarrassment! These babies are nothing to do with me. I don't want to have anything to do with them – ever!" Gary said.

"Let's leave it for now," Mum said, stroking Gary's back.

"You've spoiled everything!" Gary said.

"We'll talk about it some more in the morning," Dad said. "But right now, I'll fix your curtain." He worked in complete silence as they all tried to come to terms with Gary's reaction.

When he'd finished, Mum and Dad stood beside Gary's bed. "Goodnight," they said together and closed the door behind them.

Gary didn't reply. It wasn't a good night. It was a very bad one and he had some writing to do.

POSTCARD

Dear Father Colum,
I have some really bad news. I prayed about this and me
and Robert did what you said – we tried to give God a
helping hand. Now I'm not sure if I believe in God any
more. My mum is expecting two babies – twins. I am gutted,
sick as a parrot. They are over the moon. They never listen
to me. I wanted a dog.

Yours sincerely
Gary McNab

EIGHTEEN

It didn't take long for the news to percolate through the neighbourhood. Gary told Robert at school. Robert placed his head in his hands and said, "Oh no! What are we going to do now?"

"Nothing," Gary said. "Absolutely nothing."

"Sorry," Robert said.

"It's not your fault, Robert," Gary said. "We did our best."

Robert's gran called around a few days later with a tiny cardigan and booties. "Congratulations," she said, hugging Gary's mum. "I'm delighted for all of you. Here's a little something."

"You were supposed to be on our side," Gary muttered. "Another traitor, just like Dad."

"I know, I know Gary. It's really hard for you – after all your prayers and all our plans but..."

"You were supposed to be helping us," Gary whispered, miserably.

"I did my best, Gary, didn't I?" Gran asked.

"I suppose so."

"And didn't we have great fun with our plans?" Gran added.

Gary didn't answer. He looked at Robert's gran in disbelief. It wasn't about *fun*. It was serious and their plans hadn't worked.

"I'll be busy knitting over the next few months. I absolutely *love* making things for babies. I just can't resist them!" Gran said, ignoring Gary's angry look.

"That's really good of you, Mrs Keane," Mum said. "We'll need all the help we can get."

"Things are awful expensive, Bernadette," Gran said.

"I know," Mum replied. "We've been prepared for the price of everything!"

The two women talked and talked about clothes and equipment for the new babies. Gary scowled at them.

The phone rang. "Gary!" Dad shouted. "It's for you. An old friend."

Gary dragged his feet and his body to the phone. He hoped it was Robert.

"Hello, Gary!" He recognised the voice immediately.

"Father Colum!"

"How are you in this time of crisis? Sure, it would rock a saint's faith in God," Father Colum said.

"I'm feeling terrible, Father," Gary admitted. "I'm still gutted."

"I'm not surprised, Gary. Still, how do you fancy a trip to Manchester on Saturday with your dad and Robert? Get away from the women and all the blessed baby talk..."

"I'll ask my dad," Gary said, his voice brightening for the first time in days.

"I've already spoken to your dad about it and I've taken the liberty of buying three tickets for City's cup game at United. What do you think?"

"Sound, Father Colum. Brilliant!" Gary said.

"And we'll work out just how we can get around this small problem of the twins," Father Colum said.

"Don't mention them," Gary warned.

"OK, I won't. Still, look at Mr Doyle and me,

we're twins and we're not that bad, are we?"
Father Colum joked.

Gary laughed, again for the first time in days.
He could sense his parents listening and he could
almost feel their sigh of relief.

"See you Saturday, Gary," Father Colum said.
"City for the cup!"

"Hooray, hooray, hooray, hooray Ci-ty, Ci-ty,"
Gary sang as he paced up and down the hall.

"They won't be here for another few months,
you know, Gary," Dad said.

"Who won't?"

"The twins."

"Oh them," Gary shrugged his shoulders.
"Still, we're going to see City beat United and go
all the way to Wembley," Gary said, hopefully.

"We've got a few months to get used to the
idea," Dad said.

"What – of City winning the cup?" Gary
asked.

"No! To get used to the idea of the twins," Dad
said.

The twins. Gary would never get used to the
idea. Still, City were on a roll and it looked as
though they might make it to Wembley.

Gary didn't want to think about the twins any more.

"I know how we can forget about them," Robert suggested the next day. Robert made him feel better instantly. "I've got an idea for a plan..."

Gary groaned. "Not another one!"

32, Ramsey Grove,
Leicester,
Saturday.

Dear Father Colum,

I am just writing to ask you if you would like my dad to try and get you a ticket for Wembley? He is going down to City's ground next Thursday and he will have to start queuing at about four o'clock in the morning. Mum says it won't be too cold now that it's nearly summer.

It was absolutely brilliant at the semifinal. Tyrone Bradley played a blinder, scoring two goals and making crosses for the other two. Me and Robert sang so much that our throats were sore and we couldn't talk on the coach. My dad was glad about that. The City goalie saved another penalty and the whole team was fantastic. It was the very best day of my life. When the final whistle blew I felt so, so happy. We were all over the moon. I even said Thanks to God and I'm going to pray every day until the Cup Final because I know that City have really improved since I started to pray for them. Remember when we had to write our prayers? I wrote about City because I didn't want to tell everybody about me and Robert trying to stop the babies. If I had prayed for that, City would not be at the final. My dad says that you can't have everything in life the way that you want it. I am glad that City have got to the final for only the second time in history.

Tessie's mum is much better. She has passed lots of baby clothes to my mum but my mum thinks they might both be girls. I hope not. Mum and Dad say that I can choose one of their names. I really like Tyrone. It goes with McNab doesn't it? Tyrone McNab. Tyrone McNab. I am not sure if Mum and Dad will use my choice. We have only got four weeks left to find out. I've been thinking about what you said on the phone about you and Mr

Doyle being twins. Perhaps it won't be so bad after all.

Me and Robert are going to work out some plans to keep us away from all the hard work when Tyrone and Rosie are born. Robert is brilliant at plans. I'm glad he's my best friend. Mum says she would like Robert's gran to be a Godmother because she's been so kind to me and she's made lots of clothes for the new babies. She can also make the Christening cake because she's brilliant at cakes.

Hope you can come to the final, Father Colum, and I hope City win. Then all my prayers will be answered. Well, nearly all.

Yours sincerely,

Gary McNab.

THE DADHUNTERS

Wanted: New Dad, MUST like football!

Gary and his dad share a passionate love for football and they never miss a City match. When Gary's dad announces he is going to re-marry, Gary thinks that he will never see him or a City match again.

Gary confides in his best friend, Robert, and together they decide to find him a new football-crazy dad. Who better than local football hero, Tyrone Bradley? The only problem is how to get his mum to meet Tyrone. Then Robert has an idea...

0 00 675178-4
£3.99